PUFFIN BOOKS

LITTLE DOG LOST

Pepito, a small, funny-looking black and white puppy, lives in an old soap powder box amidst the hubbub of a Spanish fruit market – until the day the rubbish collectors come to clean up the square. Poor Pepito is too scared to move, and when he does emerge from his cardboard home he finds himself dumped at the bottom of a disused quarry, miles outside the town!

Abandoned and all alone, his exciting adventures are about to begin. During his travels he encounters all sorts of dangers and makes some friends too. But what he is really searching for is a loving and permanent home. When and where will he find one?

Little Dog Lost is a touching, amusing story by the author of the bestselling *The Snow Kitten*.

Illustrated by Terry Riley

Nina Warner Hooke

LITTLE DOG LOST

*The Life and Adventures
of Pepito*

Puffin Books

Puffin Books, Penguin Books Ltd, Harmondsworth, Middlesex, England
Penguin Viking Inc., 40 West 23rd Street, New York, New York 10010, U.S.A.
Penguin Books Australia Ltd, Ringwood, Victoria, Australia
Penguin Books Canada Ltd, 2801 John Street, Markham, Ontario, Canada L3R 1B4
Penguin Books (N.Z.) Ltd, 182–190 Wairau Road, Auckland 10, New Zealand

This unabridged version first published by Methuen Children's Books Ltd 1983
Published in Puffin Books 1985
Reprinted 1986

Copyright © Nina Warner Hooke, 1978, 1983
Illustrations copyright © Paul Bonner, 1985

This story, in a greatly abridged version, was transmitted by BBC Television as a *Jackanory* serial entitled 'Pepito' in November 1978 and repeated in January 1980.

Made and printed in Great Britain by
Richard Clay (The Chaucer Press) Ltd,
Bungay, Suffolk
Set in Monophoto Ehrhardt

I

He was born in a cardboard box in a corner of the fruit market. On the box was printed in big letters the name of a popular Spanish brand of soap powder.

His mother was a small black mongrel with white patches on her head and body. His father could have been any one of a dozen dogs that had mated with her.

She was old, mangy and half-starved. In her life she had borne many litters of puppies, few of which had lived more than a few days because she had had so little milk to give them. In the present litter there had been five, of which only one seemed likely to grow to maturity. He was the one who showed his determination to survive by pushing the others out of the way and greedily sucking what milk was to be had. It was not long before he was alone in the box. By the wise laws of nature it was better that there should be one strong puppy than five weak and sickly ones.

He was black and white like his mother. Beyond that, at this early stage of his life, it was hard to tell what he was going to look like. He was just a blind, squirming bundle about the size of a young rabbit. Two things were certain – he would always be small and he would never be handsome. Already his ears were too big for his little head and his tail was no more than a ridiculous stump.

Like all puppies he slept a great deal. But even when he

5

was awake and left alone for long periods while his mother went looking for food, he never whimpered. She seemed to have instilled in him the need to lie quiet and not to attract attention. There were some rough boys who played around the market square who might have teased or harmed him. So he lay as still and quiet as a faun in a woodland glade, even when the hot sun of Spain beat down upon the open box at midday and made him miserably hot and uncomfortable. He was thankful when the sun dropped behind the church tower and made a patch of shade where he lay.

From time to time more empty boxes, together with bottles, beer cans and tattered newspapers would be thrown into the corner. One can landed in Pepito's box, almost hitting him. But in spite of his fright he made no sound. Sometimes other dogs came to look into the box hoping to find something to eat. They sniffed at the puppy but did not hurt him. They were the town strays.

His mother was not a stray. She had an owner, though she could hardly be said to have a home. She belonged to Ramirez, a marketeer, who sold sacks of onions. She did not really have a name either. Ramirez, when he took any notice of her at all, called her simply Perra, which means she-dog. He was not intentionally cruel or neglectful, but it never occurred to him to take any care of her and he never seemed to notice how thin she was. Because of the patches of mange on her back his wife would not allow her in the house. Sometimes they forgot to feed her for days on end. Then she would search for half-eaten bread rolls thrown away by the market people. They all knew her and sometimes brought her a piece of meat or sausage.

There was one old woman who regularly brought bones left over from the Sunday stew. There was not much nourishment on the bones, but gnawing them gave her pleasure. When her puppy was old enough she brought them to him to help him cut his teeth.

It was obvious to all the marketeers that she had had her litter, but no one bothered to find out where she had hidden the puppies. A few more unwanted dogs were of no interest in a town that was overrun with them.

One morning, when the puppy was about three weeks old and already weaned, Perra went to sit by the onion stall hoping that Ramirez might remember she was hungry. He had given her no food for the past two days and she had found nothing more sustaining than a bag of sodden potato chips in the gutter. She was surprised to find a stranger at the stall. He was a lanky teenager, a distant relation who had been put in charge while Ramirez was ill. The boy did not know that Ramirez had a dog and he angrily shooed her off. Perra went a little way and then came back. She crouched and whined. The boy aimed a kick at her. She could not understand why Ramirez was not there. The day could not be a Sunday because all the other stall-holders were present and the market hummed with its weekday activity.

After a while she did what she had had to do before when neglected for too long. She went to Ramirez's house to beg. The house lay at the far end of a narrow lane. It had a shabby green door with flowerpots outside full of geraniums. She scratched at the door to draw attention to herself. Nothing happened, except that some of the peeling paint fell off. She went on scratching without result.

Señora Ramirez was out. She had gone to fetch a doctor for her husband who was in bed in the upper room. It was high time that she fetched help. Ramirez seemed to have a fever. He tossed and turned; his face was red and his night-shirt soaked with perspiration. He was gabbling, but she could not understand what he was trying to say. Plainly he was very ill.

Perra was more puzzled than ever. First there was no Ramirez; now there was apparently no Señora Ramirez either. Suddenly she remembered the shed at the side of the house where the onions were stored. Perhaps they were both in there, sacking up the onions. She found the door open and crept through into the dark and musty

8

interior, looking about her. The shed was empty. While she stood, hesitant and disappointed, wondering what to do next, a sudden gust of wind blew up the street and slammed the door shut. The latch dropped into place.

Perra sensed immediately that she was trapped. She hurled herself against the door over and over again, barking and whining, desperate to get out.

No one came to release her until long after nightfall. The people who lived in the street were so used to barking dogs that they took no notice of the noise coming from the shed.

After the doctor's visit Ramirez had fallen into an exhausted sleep. His wife was worn out also and needed rest herself. For the first time she became conscious of the barking. In her worry about Ramirez and the many things she had to do for him she had not been really aware of it. Guessing, correctly, that a local dog had got shut in the shed she came down in her dressing gown and looked through the window.

It did not surprise her to see Perra there. The poor creature was probably hungry. Señora Ramirez remembered the plates of food she had prepared for her husband, hoping to tempt him to eat. He had refused everything, wanting only water to quench his thirst. She decided to give the food to the dog – but had no chance to carry out her intention. As soon as the door was opened Perra shot out and ran off up the street as fast as her stiff old legs would carry her. Her own hunger was forgotten. All she could think about was the puppy, left alone and crying for her, all those hours. Through the back streets and across the main road she ran until she was back in the market square, making for the corner where the boxes were piled. To her consternation they were no longer there.

The rubbish collectors had been busy cleaning up the market area during her absence. The lorry came daily but usually the men left that corner untouched because the stall-holders often needed empty boxes in which to take away unsold fruit and vegetables. Today, however, instructions had been given that the whole place was to be tidied up and *all* the rubbish removed – perishable and otherwise.

At first, the puppy was not frightened by the noise of the lorry for he heard it every morning; but never before had it sounded so near to where he lay. And it was coming nearer. Louder and louder grew the roaring noise and the shouts of the men as they manoeuvred the vehicle into position and backed it into the corner. Now very frightened, the puppy tried to climb out of the box to get away from this roaring menace, but the box was too deep, his little legs could not manage it. He fell back and crawled underneath the old sack Perra had brought to make a bed for him. He was too frightened to cry. But any sound he might have made would not have been heard in that din.

Suddenly he felt the box move. He was jolted violently from side to side as it was dragged out and thrown into the truck. Other objects were tossed on top of it and presently the engine revved up and the vehicle moved off through the town and on to the highway, headed for the municipal tip. This was a disused quarry which was slowly being filled with rubbish and rubble so that the site could be put to some useful purpose. It lay some miles to the west of the town, in hilly wild country fringing the farmlands.

Reaching the turning, the lorry swerved off the highway on to the bumpy track leading to the quarry. Here it was edged to the brink, the driver pulled a lever, the tipping mechanism came into play and the whole load shot off into the pit.

The puppy did not move until the sound of the departing truck had died away in the distance. In fact he could not at first, for there was too much on top of him. Had the load been of a more solid nature he might well have been crushed to death. But cardboard cartons, empty tins and cabbage leaves are not heavy and when all was quiet again he began to try to get out. The box had fallen on its side and once he had wriggled free of the old sack he was able to leave it if he wanted to. He didn't know whether he wanted to or not. Something strange and terrible had happened to it but the box was still his only home, smelling of his mother. He was afraid to go, so he stayed where he was for a long time, whimpering loudly in his bewilderment and distress.

The very silence was frightening after the hubbub of the market. He could hear nothing but the cooing of a pigeon somewhere close by. He wondered what it was. The only birds he had heard were canaries on the balconies of houses adjoining the market. The cooing stopped when a chill wind blew over the tip, tossing the rubbish about and rattling the empty tins.

Many hours passed. When darkness fell he could bear his loneliness no longer. He wanted his mother. Since she would not, or could not, answer his cries and come to him he must go and find her.

He scrambled out of the box and was immediately totally lost amidst the rubbish. Without any idea of where to go he pushed his way forward, clambering over the larger obstacles and falling over small ones, burrowing like a mole through heaps of old newspapers and rags and broken bottles, sometimes coming up against something too large to surmount which forced him to go back and find a way round it.

Somehow or other, this erratic course brought him to the far side of the quarry where bulky objects such as worn-out refrigerators, rusty boilers and gas stoves, not included among household rubbish, were dumped in a separate place. Among them was a section of concrete drainpipe which had been rejected as imperfect when the town's new sewage system was installed. In the starlight that lit up the dismal scene the puppy saw in front of him the dark open mouth of the drainpipe and, without hesitation, he crawled into it like a wounded mouse into a hole. It offered at least a refuge from the cold wind.

In the pitch darkness he could see nothing. There was a strange smell, but his nose had been assailed by odours of so many kinds while he lay on the tip that it did not deter him. He groped forward until his nose touched something soft and furry. Whimpering joyfully he pushed up against it with the last of his strength. Here was warmth, comfort, food. He had found her. He was safe.

And then suddenly something seemed to explode in the blackness with a dreadful hissing, screeching noise. The puppy felt sharp teeth fasten on his ear. He could not retreat. He lay helpless, awaiting the full brunt of the onslaught. It did not come. The occupant of the tunnel, whatever it was, withdrew its teeth and backed away, hissing and spitting.

It was not, of course, his mother the puppy had encountered. It was a big ginger-coloured tom cat who had lived in the vicinity of the tip for most of his life. His former home had been in a hollow tree, but the tree had blown down in a winter gale and the cat had slept rough until he found the discarded drainpipe which offered a fine safe lair.

The touch of the puppy's nose awakened him from a deep sleep and at first he was almost as alarmed as the intruder. Its smell was familiar to him for in his early days he had been a farm cat, brought up with dogs and unafraid of them till the day when a newly acquired greyhound attacked and drove him away. He had not suffered in the least from this change of circumstance, in fact was far happier living wild than he had ever been at the farm, for he was well able to take care of himself.

The rats that lived on the tip provided him with his basic fare and he varied his diet with birds, lizards and beetles. At discreet intervals he raided the pigeon loft at the farm or stole a young chick from the henhouse. He was too cunning to do this very often. The farmer set a trap for him, but it was a clumsy contrivance and totally ineffective. The raider treated it with the contempt it deserved.

Over the years he had grown exceptionally big and strong and was a formidable animal to encounter – three times the size of the puppy, which he could have killed with ease. Had it tried to defend itself he would probably have done so. But it lay passive and trembling. No amount of threats and hissing made it move, and after a while the cat abandoned his efforts to drive out this invader of his home. He crouched and glared, fur raised and ears flattened with rage, at the small inert form whose outline he could just make out against the starlit mouth of the tunnel.

For a long time the two animals faced each other, neither one making a move, and gradually the cat's anger subsided. He lay down and went to sleep again – for the simple reason that no other course of action suggested itself in this baffling situation. While he slept the puppy crept up close again. Huddled against the warm fur, its body presently ceased trembling. Soon both occupants of the drainpipe were asleep.

2

The morning sun shone right into the entrance. Only the puppy was there now, the cat having slipped out before dawn to hunt. He returned with a rat dangling from his jaws. It was a large one with long yellow teeth and would have been too much for any scrawny underfed farm cat to kill, but not for the ginger tom. At the farm he had been called 'Tigre' – solely because of his colouring and not for any more suitable reason. 'Tigre', of course, is Spanish for 'tiger'. Only when he went wild and developed his size and strength was he entitled to the name. Now he was indeed a miniature tiger. No rat was too big for him to tackle.

He bit the head off the one he had caught and began to eat. The puppy heard the crunching sound and smelt the meat. He crept to the entrance and whimpered piteously. In the light of day he was a sorry sight, his coat fouled with muck, his ear bleeding and his pads cut by broken glass.

Tigre ignored his cries and calmly continued his meal. When he had had enough he stretched himself and walked away, leaving the rest of the carcase. Inch by inch the puppy crawled closer until he could reach the remains. He had tasted meat already for his mother was sometimes thrown scraps of offal by the butcher in the market. He was ravenous.

Tigre, having meticulously washed his paws and one hind leg, watched the puppy worrying the meat with his tiny teeth. When nothing was left of the rat but its tail the puppy came and sat down beside the cat, no longer afraid. Tigre washed his other hind leg. Next he stretched out his head and licked the blood off the puppy's nose. Having started on the task he decided to finish it. He licked the bitten ear and the sore little pads and he cleaned off the muck. The regular strokes of his rough tongue soothed the puppy like the caresses of his mother. Tigre, for his part, was finding something curiously pleasant in the warmth and softness of the somnolent puppy. He curled up beside it and they both took a nap in the sunshine.

So began the strange partnership that was to last for the next year and a half.

Tigre was a fine hunter and never went short of a meal. Invariably he brought his prey home and left a portion of it for his companion. When the puppy grew bigger and more active he was sometimes allowed to accompany Tigre and he learned a lot from watching the big cat make his kill. But it was a long while before he was able to kill a rat by himself. He knew what to do but was not yet able to do it. He had to grow to his proper size and discipline his muscles before he could achieve the deadly spring and quick bite at the back of the neck which was necessary. While learning, he was bitten several times. The big rats were brave and defended themselves fiercely. Mice were easier to catch and less dangerous. He had more luck with them and grew careless. Consequently he was greatly surprised when a mouse that he had caught nipped him sharply on the nose. He yelped with indignation and thereafter took more care.

Success came with maturity and practice. He was, after all, more of a terrier than anything else and all terriers are natural ratters. By the time he was eight months old and full grown he was as skilful a hunter as Tigre and had even, with Tigre's help, caught a few rooks and pigeons – some while they were roosting and some when they were actually in flight. To accomplish this feat the two animals had to hunt as a team. They discovered how to do it by accident.

Tigre had been stalking a rook that was probing for worms in a patch of loose earth. He thought his friend was following him but the little dog had stopped to sniff at something behind a briar bush. The rook saw the cat, turned and flapped into the air, its flight taking it directly over the briar bush. Instinctively the dog leapt up. His legs were short but well muscled and the leap took him high enough to grab the rook by the tail. Some of the feathers came away but the rest held and the rook fell heavily to the ground where Tigre pounced on it. A quick snap of the dog's jaws put an end to its struggles.

The two hunters contemplated their catch with some pride. They used this tactic often after that, one partner driving the prey into the path of the other, as lions and wolves do.

Their life was not altogether carefree. At regular intervals the garbage truck arrived with a fresh load which was tipped on to the dump. When this happened the landscape was changed for the occupants of the drainpipe. More than once the pipe itself was engulfed as the level rose and they had to dig themselves out through a barrier of assorted rubbish.

They were reluctant to leave their home for no better refuge could have been found than this snug tunnel with an exit at both ends. There came a time when they were specially thankful for this facility.

Rabbits were scarce in that dry rocky country and were hardly ever seen. The two friends had caught only one during their partnership. But a few telltale droppings were spotted one day by one of the garbage men on the hillside above the quarry. That weekend he and his friends from local farms formed a shooting party. Three men with guns and half a dozen rangy hounds scrambled up and down. The air resounded with yelps, shouts and random shots. The hunt ended when one man fell off a rock, twisted his ankle and had to be carried away by the other two. The hounds, untrained and disobedient, kept tethered for most of their wretched lives, raced about barking ecstatically. They caught no rabbits but made the most of every minute of their freedom. They were tall, pale-coloured hounds with sharp muzzles and long thin tails, savage from underfeeding and confinement, not gifted with much intelligence but good trackers.

One of them picked up Tigre's scent and it led him to the mouth of the drainpipe. Two others joined him and they milled about outside, baying furiously but unable to get in because of their size.

Tigre and his friend lay very quiet, their hearts thumping. In their tunnel they were safe. But Tigre knew that where there were hounds there were always men with guns. The noise the hounds were now making would bring the men back and they would find means of driving him into the open. Having been shot at more than once he could not control his agitation but stole out of the other end of the pipe and dashed up the quarry slope. None of the hounds suspected that the tunnel had a rear exit. They continued to bark and bay at the front until one of them caught a flying glimpse of reddish fur high up the slope and hurled itself in pursuit. The rest soon followed. Any of them would have killed Tigre if they had overtaken him, but by now the cat had reached the safety of the trees. He darted up the nearest pine trunk and sat tight in a fork of the branches, glaring at his pursuers. It was lucky for him that there had been an accident to the shooting party. He would have been an easy target if the men had still been around, for his colouring made him conspicuous against the dark pine needles.

After a while the hounds tired of the sport and wandered off. Presently their owners could be heard calling and whistling them. At last all was quiet again. But Tigre did not descend until half an hour had passed and he was sure that all pursuit had ceased. He came back to find his companion lying where he had left him. The little dog had shown more sense than Tigre on this occasion.

Usually, however, it was Tigre who made the wise decisions and chose their daily course of action, he who found water for them to drink in dry periods and new litters of young rats and mice that made delicious eating. The little dog had respect and affection for the friend who had taken the place of his mother.

They did not spend all their time together. He wandered off alone sometimes to explore the pine woods above the quarry. Summer had ended and in the cool days of autumn it was pleasant to play with fir cones and chase lizards.

Tigre, for his part, disappeared quite often too on private business, staying away for several days while he paid court to one of the female cats in the district. But at all other times the dog and the cat curled up together every night keeping each other warm.

Tigre's raids on the pigeon loft at the farm had become more frequent recently. He was tired of a diet of rodent flesh and hungered for tastier fare. His appetite was his undoing. The day came when he did not return from one of these expeditions.

The loft was built on the roof of the farmhouse. His strategy was to take up his position before dawn on the guttering below the eaves and wait till the pigeons took their morning flight at sunrise. When the first bird stepped out through the narrow door to preen itself before taking off he would spring from his hiding place, seize it, jump down on to the water butt and thence to the ground and away – so fast that even when he was spotted, as sometimes happened, no one could stop him. He was hundreds of yards away before the farmer could go for his gun or untie the dogs. He was adept at evading any hounds that chased him, by simply obliterating his trail. He would make for a patch of low-lying swampy land in the opposite direction from the quarry tip. The tussocks of reeds and rushes would bear a cat but would not support the heavy hounds who floundered miserably about in the murky water trying to pick up his scent.

On this occasion things went wrong for Tigre. He failed to kill the pigeon when he caught it and it was jerking between his teeth when he jumped from the guttering. He knew that the old worm-eaten lid of the water butt was unsafe and he was always careful to land on the edge where it was supported by the rim of the barrel. Hampered by the struggling bird he jumped short, landing right in the middle where the wood was most rotten. The lid caved in. The butt chanced to be three parts full after a recent rainstorm. Tigre was drowned.

The little dog was not at first distressed by his friend's

failure to return. He was accustomed to the cat's absences on hunting and courting expeditions. But after five days had passed he began to suspect that all was not as it should be. At the end of a week he was certain of it. He slept in fits and starts, listening for Tigre's stealthy tread and waiting for the warm pressure of the furry form against his own. He shivered a lot during this fitful sleep for it was full winter now and the nights were cold. Very often it rained and, when he emerged from the tunnel, it was to see a dismal, uninviting scene around him.

His hunting became so half-hearted that he often went hungry. On some days he did not hunt at all but went off looking for Tigre. He searched the pine woods above, the crevices of the quarry walls, all the places they had frequented together, barking and whining to announce his presence and always hoping for an answering cry. None ever came. There was only silence and the rain dripping from the trees. He would wander back to the drainpipe, bedraggled and despondent, curl up into a tight black and white ball and try to keep warm.

During the next few weeks his unhappiness grew more and more unbearable. He wanted to leave this place, for it was no longer a home to him without Tigre, but he knew no other. He had never ranged far afield as Tigre had done. The area of the quarry was all he knew. His origins in the market place of the town had long ago faded from his mind.

One fine, bright morning in early spring he crept out of the drainpipe, shook himself and set off without looking back at the place where he had lived since he was three weeks old. He had no idea where to go. One direction was as good as another. After some slight hesitation he chose the wild country east of the quarry, stopped to catch a couple of woodmice for his breakfast and then followed an old overgrown track that led him to some rough pasture where goats were grazing. He gave them a wide berth for his only previous encounter with a goat was when the old billy at the farm had broken his tether, wandered down to the quarry and charged him on sight. The dog was far more agile than the goat and easily escaped the sharp horns, but it had given him a fright. These were she-goats however and they were as wary of him as he was of them. One had a young kid, pretty and playful, skipping about her legs and butting her sides. They watched him suspiciously as he crossed the pasture.

He came to a low hill from which he could see a white building set in a grove of almond trees. It was an old dilapidated farmhouse, the limewash peeling off its walls, the fence broken and the garden rank with weeds. It looked as if it had been deserted for many years, as was in fact the case; but there was evidence that somebody lived there now, had perhaps just moved in. Smoke came from the crooked chimney and a washing line had been strung between two almond trees. The grass had been cut on a small patch of ground outside the front door. On the step lay three cats, sunning themselves.

The new occupants were a young English couple, Trevor and Julia Martin, who had rented the place for the summer. It was cheap and they were prepared to work hard to make it passably habitable. Both were artists, Julia a painter and Trevor a sculptor in wood.

The house contained some shabby bits of furniture and

a rusty stove to cook on. There was a well from which to draw water, but no other amenities. The young couple did not mind such primitive conditions. To spend a summer in Spain was a novel and exciting experience for which they had been saving money since they were married. They accepted the hardships, the lack of electric light, the long distance to the nearest shop, without complaint, as they accepted the cats who lived there.

3

They first noticed the new arrival when they were trying to hang the gate back on its hinges. Lying in the shade of a fig tree, watching them with bright curious eyes, was a small black and white dog. The next day he was still there, still watching, but never coming any nearer. If they approached him he shrank away, showing his teeth. They couldn't understand why he was so nervous.

'He must have been ill-treated, poor little thing,' said Julia. 'But he doesn't look in poor condition. In fact he looks remarkably healthy.'

The truth, though they would have found it hard to believe, was that they were the only people this dog had ever met, other than the refuse collectors whom he had seen from a distance discharging their load, and the occasional figure of a rabbit hunter in the pine woods. He was to all intents and purposes a wild animal and as shy as any other creature of the wild. He was not afraid of these two, for his instinct told him they meant no harm; but he could not bring himself yet to respond to their friendly advances.

He liked the cats – who did not repulse him because they smelt Tigre's scent on him. He soon discovered that they slept in the old shed at the back of the house where Julia had spread a blanket for them.

Trevor went in one morning to fetch a slab of olive

wood he had stored there and came out smiling broadly. 'He sleeps in there with the cats,' he told Julia.

'See if you can coax him out.'

Trevor hesitated. 'Do we really want to make a pet of him? I mean, the cats are no trouble, they can look after themselves. But a dog needs feeding.'

'He won't eat much. He's very small and there are always left-overs. Here, give him this piece of tortilla. If he's a stray he'll eat anything.'

Once again they were in for a surprise. When Trevor put the offering down in front of him the little dog came up and sniffed at it, then turned away in disgust. Accustomed to eating raw flesh he didn't know what to make of this pancake of egg, onion and potato.

'Well, if it's meat he wants he'll have to go without,' Julia said. 'We can't explain to him that we're vegetarians. Maybe we'd better not encourage him to stay around and before long he'll go off to find a more suitable home.'

They offered him nothing more and steeled themselves to take no notice of him. But their indifference had no effect. He continued to stay, watching with the greatest interest their comings and goings and everything they did. Sometimes, when they were busy, he would steal a little nearer, but would crouch on his belly if they looked round and saw him.

The young couple had settled in. They had cleaned out the house and made it as comfortable as they could with the meagre furnishings. Julia had hung cheap cotton curtains at the windows and Trevor had made a work bench out of some old planks on which he set out his carving tools each morning. Julia bought canvases and painted the old house from all angles. She loved it, from its pantiled roof and peeling walls to the unpruned vine that clambered over the remains of the pergola. The almond trees had shed their blossoms and the boughs were laden with hard little green nuts. Opposite the front door was a lemon tree in full flower; its perfume wafted about her as she worked. 'One day when we're rich,' she told Trevor, 'we'll come back and buy this place and restore it and put in a bathroom and plant a garden and . . .'

'When that day comes,' said Trevor with a chuckle, 'we'll probably be too old to tackle such a job. Anyway I like it as it is.'

They were very happy. Only one thing troubled them. Adjoining the house were some outbuildings, a stable and a pigsty. The owner of the house was an old man who lived alone in a shabby cottage nearby. He kept goats and raised a few crops of potatoes and carrots which he stored in the stable along with maize cobs and locust beans. He turned up at regular intervals to help himself to these stores – and was not the only one to do so. The store supported numbers of rats. Years of good living had increased their size. They were nearly as big as the undersized cats who left them severely alone. When the she-cats had kittens the rats killed and ate them. They roamed freely about the house and garden, showing little fear of the occupants. Julia was terrified of them. She would not go into the outbuildings alone. This was the only thing that marred their happiness and she tried not to think about it by concentrating on her work.

While she painted she was often conscious, now, of the small silent onlooker lying under the fig tree close by.

Every time she turned her head she found the bright alert gaze fixed on her. Four days had passed since the dog arrived.

'He's still here,' she called to Trevor who was working at his bench round the corner. 'What are we going to do about him?'

'Why, nothing. He'll go away eventually,' Trevor called back.

'What do you think he's living on?'

'Who knows?'

They were soon to find out.

Their hired motorcycle was kept in the stable when not in use. The building had a heavy door which was pad-locked at night. Had the machine been stolen it would have meant a serious loss to the young couple. One night Trevor forgot to lock the door. When he went to fetch the motorcycle next morning for a shopping trip into the town he found four huge rats, one of them half eaten, laid out on the floor. He shouted to Julia.

'Good heavens! Julie, come and look at this.'

Julia came running from the house and they both stood and stared.

'It's that dog. It must be. He's an expert ratter.'

'Well, that settles it. He can stay here as long as he likes, bless him.'

'He's watching – look, and wagging his tail. I believe he's asking if we're pleased.'

From that time he was adopted into the family. He was their dog, even though they could not fondle him. No human hand had ever touched him and he still would not allow it. But he would come and sit beside them and he responded when they talked to him. Little by little he was becoming domesticated. After the first week or so he permitted himself to be stroked – and found that he enjoyed the sensation so much that he wanted more. The day came when they were able to pick him up. He would even eat the scraps they gave him, because he saw that it gave them pleasure to feed him; although he supported himself almost entirely on rats.

Several times they watched him catching them, saw how cleverly he stalked them, pouncing like lightning, killing with one bite and tossing them in the air. The rat population had diminished very noticeably and none was ever seen in the house now.

Julia was no longer nervous. When she went into the

stable the dog went with her, her guard and protector.

He was a real pet dog now. He had a home, fond owners and even a name. They called him Pepito. As looks went, he was hardly a pet to be proud of. His ears were too big for his body. The right one had never recovered from Tigre's bite and had a permanent droop. His tail was a mere stump. But 'handsome is as handsome does,' Trevor said; and Pepito was earning more than his keep.

Though given the run of the house he preferred to sleep in the shed with the cats. They were all friendly and filled the gap in his life left by Tigre.

Contented though he was with his new life he still had a streak of wildness which showed itself in independence. He did as he liked, sometimes following Julia when she went off somewhere to paint, sometimes staying behind with Trevor. He went off alone on hunting or exploring trips but seldom stayed away from the house for more than a few hours. When Trevor rode to the nearest tienda, or into the town, to do the household shopping, Pepito often accompanied him, sitting in a box strapped to the pillion seat and showing no fear of passing traffic. But if he did not want to come, no amount of calling and whistling would make him.

Every afternoon he took his siesta under the fig tree. Julia painted him lying there with his head on his paws. He had all but forgotten his former life and no longer pined for Tigre. He was perfectly happy.

The same could not be said of the young couple. They had grown very attached to Pepito and before them loomed the problem of what they were to do with him when the time came to return to England. Already it was September. They were coming to the end of their tenancy and their money. Trevor had to go back to get a job. Julia's mother was not well and she worried about her.

'If only we could take him with us!'

'We can't; you know that, not without putting him in quarantine for six months. And that's a very expensive business.'

'Couldn't we smuggle him? He's so small and he hardly ever barks . . .'

'Much too dangerous. You can be fined hundreds of pounds for breaking quarantine laws.'

'Other countries don't have them.'

'Other countries aren't kept free of rabies like England. It's a horrible disease.'

'Well then, what are we going to do? We can't just *leave* him.'

'I don't see any alternative, unless we can find him a home with some other people.'

'We don't know any other people except farmers and shopkeepers and they've all got dogs of their own.'

'Perhaps he'll go back where he came from. He must have *had* a home –'

'He wouldn't have come to us if he'd had a good one, would he?'

'No. Oh lord, I don't know what to do about him.'

In the end they did the only thing they could think of. On the day before their departure they rode into town to return the motorcycle and arrange for a taxi to collect them and their belongings from the farmhouse. They had now, besides their personal things, a collection of Trevor's carvings which were to be exhibited in London and several of Julia's paintings. Then they went to the town hall and asked to speak to the Mayor. After waiting some time they were shown into his office. He proved to be a pleasant elderly man who spoke good English and seemed ready enough to help them if he could. But it was soon clear that he could do nothing.

'I'm sorry, señores, we have no facilities here for the care of unwanted animals.'

'But that's terrible,' Julia said. 'Is there nowhere at all?'

'Maybe in Madrid and in bigger towns than ours. Here we have nothing.'

'But we simply can't go off and leave this poor little dog, who has been our pet and our friend for six months, without providing for him.'

'You cannot take him to England?'

'No, it's impossible.'

'Other foreign tourists, Germans and French, take home their pets.'

'They don't have strict quarantine laws like we do.'

'Couldn't we –' Julia looked beseechingly at him. He had a kind face. 'Could we leave him at the police station, do you think?'

The Mayor laughed ruefully. 'Señora, if you did so, they would just turn him into the street. What else could they do? If you take my advice you will do the same. You worry too much. He will not starve. There are always people who give food to the strays – mistakenly, in our view. We have too many stray dogs. Something will have to be done about them before long. They foul our streets and cause traffic accidents.'

Sadly the Martins made their way to the bus stop. Back at the house they packed their things and tidied up, too upset to talk much. Pepito followed them around all the time, watchful and uneasy. He sensed that a radical change was imminent and that it was affecting his friends. He tried to show his concern for them by rubbing against their legs. It was the only way he knew of showing his affection.

The next day dawned and the taxi came to take Julia and Trevor to the airport. Their suitcases and the box with the carvings and paintings were loaded up; the house door was locked and the key hung on a nail in the woodshed as arranged. They had left a big meal for the cats and filled the water bowl. Pepito they took with them. He sat between them on the back seat. They told the driver to stop in the main square of the town for a few minutes. Here they both got out. Trevor held Pepito in his arms. Julia took from her shoulder bag a piece of brown ribbon she had pulled from one of her dresses. On this she had fixed with paper clips a card on which she had printed in Spanish:

HIS NAME IS PEPITO.
PLEASE BE KIND TO HIM.

She tied the ribbon around his neck, hugged him and kissed him and set him down on the pavement. Then they both got back into the taxi. Julia was crying as it drove off through the town.

*

Late that night when they were back in their flat near London and had unpacked their things Julia hung her painting of Pepito on the wall of the living room. But she found that it upset her too much to have the small shaggy white face looking at her, as it used to do so often when she was working, and she took the picture down and put it away.

4

For some time after the taxi had driven away Pepito sat on the pavement where he had been left, waiting to be collected again. He had not been nervous during the drive for he was used to the noise of the petrol engine and had ridden in a taxi once before when Trevor had taken some of his larger carvings to a shop in the town for sale. The packing of suitcases and loading of luggage into the vehicle had not alarmed him. He had not been domesticated for long enough to know that such actions are the inevitable signs of human departure.

Without any sense of foreboding therefore he stayed where he was for an hour or more. The square was full of traffic, honking and roaring in all directions. People ran across roads, flocked in and out of shops, hurried by with bags and parcels and prams. He had not known there could be so many people in the world. Some nearly fell over him. One man, carrying trays of tomatoes into a supermarket, kicked him out of the way. He scuttled down a side street and here, where it was quieter, he sat down again to wait. But he was growing worried now, worried and bewildered, uttering an occasional whine to express his feelings. Several people noticed him. A priest stooped down to look at the card attached to the ribbon. 'Poor little chap,' he said, and, with a helpful shrug of his shoulders, walked on. A little boy offered a biscuit. Pepito ignored it. He did not want food, he wanted his friends to come back and fetch him.

As the day wore on the conviction grew in his mind that it was no use staying here any longer. They must have gone back to the house and be waiting there for *him*. Having formed a decision he trotted off at once, choosing by instinct the right direction to take out of the town.

By the following day, using the marvellous means some animals possess of returning home unaided over long distances, he had found his way back. It was a journey of some eight or nine miles mostly over rough country, for he did not follow the roadway. He went in a more or less straight line through fields and farms and stony tracts of scrubland, always guided by the mysterious compass in his head, to the grassy rise from which he could see the farmhouse lying before him.

He knew when he approached it that something had happened. There was no sound of voices. All the doors and windows were closed and the shutters fastened. Gone were the familiar washing line and the bowl outside the back door where Trevor scraped the potatoes. The cats welcomed him back but Pepito was too distressed to return their greeting. He ran round the house barking frantically and scratching at the doors.

He had sense enough to realize after a short time that all this effort was futile. They were not there, so much was clear. Therefore they must be where he had last seen them, in the town, and in due course they would come home as they always did after their shopping trips. He had only to wait and presently he would hear the noise of the motor bike bumping along the track from the main road. For the rest of the day he lay in his customary place under the fig tree. When night fell he was still there; but by dawn he knew that they were not coming back to the house and he set off to look for them in the town.

For the next two days he wandered about the streets. By now he was very hungry. Rats were scarce in the town at this time for there had recently been a campaign to get rid of them by putting out poisoned bait. It took Pepito several hours to catch a young one coming out of a sewer pipe.

The tantalizing smells coming from cafés, hamburger stands and restaurants drew him irresistibly, but he was soon to discover that he trespassed at his peril in the vicinity of these places. Every eating place had its band of canine hangers-on, always prowling hopefully around or sitting under the tables, and fiercely resentful of interlopers. These packs of street dogs had increased over the last few years when this part of Spain had begun to be popular with tourists. The foreigners fed the dogs, and the Spaniards – taking their cue from their customers – began to be more tolerant towards the strays. The authorities did not like them and there were rumours that steps were to be taken to deal with them 'on higher orders'. In the meantime the street gangs lived reasonably well. In winter when the eating places were mostly closed they raided dustbins and stole from market stalls when opportunity occurred.

Pepito had to fight hard for acceptance into one of these bands. His smallness was against him and if he had been other than he was, he might never have achieved it at all and might have died of starvation.

He had plenty of courage and his training as a hunter under Tigre stood him in good stead. He was so agile and quick that he could get in several bites before a bigger dog could seize and hold him. After a few weeks, during which he had many fights and was often quite painfully hurt but had never run away, he began to be known and respected.

And so began another chapter of his eventful life.

He had joined the pack attached to the Bar Toro, a prosperous establishment not far off the main square. It was a cafeteria as well as a bar, where light meals could be had at all hours, and was popular with both tourists and townspeople on account of its pleasant situation. In front was a big paved terrace shaded by acacia trees under which the tables were set out.

Papa Romero, the owner, was a big jovial man who had been a promising matador until he was wounded in a bullfight in Madrid. He and his wife did the cooking. Mama Dolores was as big as he was, with a fierce temper and great brawny arms like a man's. In hot weather Papa worked shirtless and fans of the bullfight would flock into the kitchen to look at the great scar down one side of his body where the bull had gored him.

It was a family business. The two waiters, Toni and Ramon, were nephews and there was a thin, tired-looking cousin called Conchita who did the cleaning and washing up.

Mama Dolores, despite her forbidding looks, was soft-hearted and once a day she filled a bucket with scrapings from the plates and took it out to her 'pobrecitos', as she called them. It amused her that these homeless dogs had a rigid order of precedence. The leader had his turn first. Then came the senior members of the group. By the time it was Pepito's turn there was not much left in the bucket but slops – sometimes nothing at all. But there was generally something to be picked up under the tables and he had learned quickly that people found him appealing when he sat and gazed at them with his bright black eyes, one ear up and one down, and they would throw him a tasty morsel.

The neck ribbon with Julia's message on it had vanished long ago, torn off in a fight. He had as yet no special identity. He was just a newcomer to the pack, until one

39

chilly day a priest came in for a cup of coffee to warm him up. It was he who had noticed the small lost dog in the side street not long before.

'How long has that one been around?' he asked Toni. Toni shrugged.

'I don't know. A week or so, I think. Not long.'

'I recognize him,' said the priest. 'I can't tell you where he comes from or anything else about him, but his name is Pepito.' And he described how he had stooped to read the words on the card.

'The others gave him a bad time at first,' said Toni. 'But he held his own and now they seem to have accepted him. He has plenty of guts, I'll say that for him.'

'He looks intelligent too. A nice little dog.'

'So far as I'm concerned,' said Toni, 'he's just one more nuisance about the place and I wish he'd gone elsewhere.' The waiters disliked the dogs who were always getting under their feet at busy times. But the customers liked them; the regular ones knew many animals individually and reserved special titbits for their favourites. The dogs were as much a feature of the place as the tiled terrace and the acacia trees.

Pepito had not settled down quickly to his new way of life as a street dog, for he had been constantly pulled in two directions. Had he been left by the Martins in the country he would probably have stayed there and reverted to the wild. But he had last seen them in the town and it was here that he was always hoping to find them again.

From time to time he was drawn back to the farmhouse to make sure they had not returned; and once there, he

usually stayed for a few days. It was still empty and
deserted. Grass and weeds had grown tall. The pergola
had fallen down and the vine lay in a tangle among docks
and thistles, the unpicked grapes withered and flyblown.
The gate was off its hinges again. It was a sad-looking
place.

There were only two cats now, as one of the females
had died. But several half-grown kittens augmented the
family. The kittens always rushed away when they saw
Pepito, but the others were glad to see him. The stores of
potatoes and beans in the stable had all been consumed or
removed by the farmer, so the rats were no longer numer-
ous enough to menace the kittens.

Pepito discovered during these visits that he had lost
his appetite for rodent flesh and he was glad to return to
the Bar Toro. He had grown to like the varied diet of
table scraps, chicken bones, fried potatoes and even bread.
Although he lost condition on this sort of fare he seldom
went hungry.

Sleeping in the open was the worst hardship, especially
in winter weather, for he was unused to it. All through the
first winter of his life he had had shelter and a warm
companion. He had to learn the best sleeping places from
the other dogs and then compete with them for a share of
the space. Once he had secured a space it remained his by
right of ownership. The place where he spent his nights
was the doorway of a bakery on the south side of the
square. It was sheltered from the wind and its deep portico
kept off the rain. He shared the doorway with two other
dogs, both mongrels like himself.

Every morning when the shop opened up they were

shooed away, but they hung about until vans arrived from the restaurants to collect the bread which had been baked during the night shift. It sometimes happened that a roll or two would fall off a tray and then there was a concerted rush for it. Pepito was so quick that he generally won the prize. After crunching the hot fresh bread he would wander off with the others to stretch his legs and then they would all make for the Bar Toro, there to spend the rest of the day.

In this way passed the next two years of his existence. It could not be said that he was unhappy. He had finally adapted himself to the conditions in which he had to live.

The Bar people were now the humans in his life, though they were never his friends in the way that Trevor and Julia had been. He had all but forgotten the Martins. It was only when customers came to the café bringing their own dogs that he felt an aching sense of loss. He saw how those dogs, the fortunate, the valued ones, sat close to their owners, responding with wagging tails and adoring eyes to the smallest caress. He remembered the warm thrill of being hugged and fondled in the days when he had 'belonged' as they did.

Occasionally someone took an active interest in him. One day a lady came in to buy ice cream for her little daughter. It was the child's birthday and she was dressed in pink, with two pink bows in her hair. 'What else would you like, darling?' asked her mother when the ice cream was finished.

'A present.'

'But you have had your presents. Lots of them. You have so many that I don't know where you will put them all. What else is it you want?'

The child pointed to Pepito, who was sitting near by. 'I want a little dog. *That* one.'

'I expect he belongs to somebody,' the lady said hopefully. Ramon, who was making out the bill at the next table, looked round and said quickly, 'No, no, he's just a street dog like the rest. Take him if you want him.'

The child's mother frowned. 'Dearest, I don't really think you want a dog to look after, do you? A dog is such a nuisance. You have a canary –'

'I do, I do. I want a little dog.'

'The apartment is not suitable. No garden for a dog to run about in. I really think it is not a good idea, darling.' The little girl was used to getting her own way and had a very effective method of achieving it. She threw a tantrum. 'I want it, I want it, I want the little dog,' she shrieked, beating on the table with her fists.

'*O madre mia!*' cried the lady, wringing her hands. 'What a way to behave on your birthday, Carmencita. Please to control yourself. Everyone is looking at us.'

'I don't care!'

In the end the lady did what she usually had to do. She gave in. Calling Ramon, she told him, 'My car is parked over there. I will go to it now and hold the door open. Will you put the dog in for me?'

Ramon accepted a generous tip, picked up Pepito and put him in the back of the car. The little girl jumped in and the door was slammed. The car drove off to a fashionable block of apartments on the outskirts of the town.

Pepito registered his protest at this strange turn of events by barking all the way. He didn't understand what was happening to him but he didn't like it. And he didn't like the little girl who sat on the back seat with him and kept trying to haul him on to her lap and pull his ears. As soon as they reached their destination he ran into the first room he came to and dived under the bed. Nothing would induce him to come out. A maid tried to push him out with a broom but he growled and bared his teeth. The little girl coaxed and cried and screamed. Food was put down for him but he refused to touch it.

After a day and a half of this the family was worn out and the whole household disrupted. The little girl's father had to take a hand. With everyone helping, Pepito was at last driven out of the bedroom where he had taken refuge. The street door was left open. Given his chance of escape he thankfully took it, scurrying back to the Bar Toro as fast as his legs would carry him.

Another offer of a home came during the following summer. This time it was not from someone who merely wanted an animated toy but from a man who needed a dog for a useful purpose.

He was a retired train driver whose garden was his pride and joy. What he required was a dog to chase cats out of it. This garden was the only open space in a heavily built-up area and was consequently the scratching ground of all the neighbourhood cats. They caught and killed the birds that nested in his apricot trees.

The idea came to him at the Bar Toro while he was drinking a beer and idly watching the dogs wandering about the terrace. 'That's what I want,' he thought. 'A dog. A dog of the terrier type. A terrier will chase anything.' He looked them over carefully. They were a motley rabble of all shapes and sizes. Some, who had survived being hit by cars, hopped on three legs. Some were too old and feeble for the job. His eye fixed on Pepito who at least looked young and healthy. He picked him up, carried him into the kitchen and asked Papa Romero, 'Can I take him?'

'Of course. Take him and a few more!'

Pepito struggled, but the man was strong and carried him through the town to his house. There he was installed in the garden with an upturned packing case for a kennel. A rope was slung across the width of the garden between the apricot trees, running through a ring attached to another piece of rope round Pepito's neck. This arrangement, while keeping the dog captive, allowed him to run from one side to the other and it provided, as the man thought, an ideal solution to the problem. Unfortunately he had overlooked one important factor. Far from driving the cats away Pepito welcomed them. He let them scratch where they would and lay down beside them when they took their naps. This adoption did not, therefore, last long. Pepito was returned in disgrace to the Bar Toro.

After this, when someone looked at him in a kindly way or made overtures of friendship, he held back, wary and suspicious. Had any other people offered to take him they would have found him very difficult to catch. He had given himself willingly to humans once, given them his love and loyalty, and they had gone away and left him. It would be a long while before he would risk it again. Although he mingled with the bar dogs, joined in their skirmishes and held his place among them, it began to be noticed that his character and behaviour were different.

He did not scramble for food that was thrown from the tables but sat apart and waited for something to be given him. Battered little outcast though he was, he had a dignity that set him apart. And all the time his sharp eyes observed people, the passers-by, the customers at the café tables. He watched their faces and movements, he listened to their voices. By this time he knew that the Martins had gone out of his life for ever. They were forgotten, but not the happiness they had given him. He had had a taste of joy and the memory of it remained inside him, a small unquenchable flame.

He watched and waited. Sooner or later, among all these hundreds of humans who came and went, there must be one to whom he could safely entrust himself and who would not misuse or reject him. And when that one came, he would look at him and he would know him immediately.

Towards the end of the summer season came the feast day of San Paulo, the town's patron saint. It was a public holiday and the most popular festival of the year. All the eating places, big and small, expected to be full. Nobody ate at home on the Feast of San Paulo. The Bar Toro was well prepared. Strings of bunting decorated the terrace and coloured lights were hung in the trees. Papa Romero had gone early to market and bought chickens, rabbits, mussels and prawns and all the other ingredients of *paella*, the dish most in demand on feast days. He had brought out the huge shallow pans in which it was cooked and was now chopping onions and sweet peppers while Conchita plucked the chickens.

Mama Dolores was baking *graixonera*, the special sweet made of cake soaked in egg and syrup for which she was famous. Toni and Ramon rushed to and from the cellar for more and more cases of red wine. The ice cream van arrived with a fresh load for the freezer. A consignment of vegetables was delivered. People kept phoning up to book tables. There was pandemonium at the Bar Toro and the dogs kept well out of the way of the rushing feet.

By twelve o'clock all the tables on the terrace were full. The procession was passing down the street bearing the effigy of the saint back to the church, held aloft by six strong men and preceded by the clergy in their colourful vestments. After them came the Boys' Club beating drums, and little girls with flowers.

The sun beat down on the crowded tables and orders were shouted from all sides. The two hard-pressed waiters rushed in and out with tubs of ice cream, cups of coffee, glasses of sherry and tall, frosted tumblers containing orange and lemon drinks.

Everyone was talking about the procession. A fat man in a check shirt leaned over to talk to the occupant of the next table, a slim young Frenchman in a T-shirt and jeans. 'Did you notice the boy carrying the banner?'

'I beg your pardon?'

'Did you see the boy with the banner?'

'Which banner? There were many.'

'The first one, the biggest. He's my son.'

'Oh, really?'

'It's heavy, you know, but he insisted.'

'He carried it well.'

'He's a fine boy. Will you take a glass of sherry with me, señor, to drink his health?'

'With pleasure.'

The young man spoke Spanish slowly and haltingly. During the conversation that ensued he explained that his name was Jean-Louis Leblanc and that he was a law student on a walking holiday. It was the first time he had visited this part of Spain, though he knew the south fairly well and had once walked from Granada over the Sierra Nevada to Almeria in a week.

'And where are you making for now, may I ask?'

'For Sanesteban, and then perhaps Pamplona.'

'Too late to see the running of the bulls.'

'No matter. There is so much else. It's the best way to see your beautiful country – and the cheapest.'

'Ah, but one must be young and fit to do it. Myself, I prefer to see it from a car. But I envy you. May you have the best holiday you ever had.'

'Thank you, señor. I hope to do so.'

While the two men were talking there was a minor disaster nearby. Toni, while hurrying by, tripped over and dropped a tray containing several orders of ice cream. Streaks of raspberry, chocolate and vanilla shot over the terrace. Kicks and curses had no effect on the rush of dogs to lick it up. The two men watched them, smiling.

'It's not often they get a treat like that,' said the fat man. 'But on the whole they do pretty well. They're strays, picking up a living as best they can. But they won't be around much longer.'

'Oh. Why is that?'

'We have regulations now for the control of stray dogs.

Every town has an official dog-catcher whose job it is to impound them. There used to be more here than you see today. Many have been rounded up already. The rest will go soon.'

Jean-Louis watched them, his young face filled with pity. Two were lame; others had sores from infected bites. He loved all animals. This was a sad sight to someone unused to it. 'What happens to them?' he asked.

'Well, they will be kept for a while in the hope that some may find a home – the better-looking ones perhaps. If they don't, they will be put to sleep. It's necessary, you see. Can't have a mob of dogs running loose in the streets nowadays. They cause too many accidents.'

By now the pavement was licked clean and the dogs were begging at the tables. There was one, however, who sat apart, Jean-Louis noticed. It was a small black and white mongrel with a stumpy tail and big ears, one of which had a permanent droop. His ribs showed under his rough and staring coat, but the eyes in his lively little face were bright as buttons. Those eyes were fixed on Jean-Louis with such intensity that he could almost feel them boring into him. He averted his own gaze and began to eat the sticky cake on his plate. He left half of it, which he broke into two pieces and held out. The stumpy tail wagged slightly but the dog did not move.

'You have to give it to him,' the fat man said. 'He won't come to you.'

'Is he frightened?'

'No. Proud, that's all – like a true Spaniard. He's telling you that he's not like the rest. He doesn't beg or do tricks, but if you have anything to spare he would be grateful for it. We all know Pepito. He's been around for some time. Some of us will be sorry to see him go.'

Jean-Louis stood up. He crossed the pavement and held out a piece of cake. The little dog did not snatch and gulp but accepted it gently and politely. His teeth were white and sharp. He didn't seem very old. Jean-Louis stooped to pat him. Then he turned away and beckoned the waiter for his bill. Pepito's eyes never left him. The young Frenchman counted out the money and then hoisted his pack on to his back and fastened the straps. All the time he was conscious of that unblinking gaze riveted upon him. 'I'll be off then,' he said to the fat man. 'Thank you for the sherry.'

'*Adios, chico*. Enjoy yourself.'

Jean-Louis took three long strides down the street. Then he stopped and looked back. Pepito's head had turned to watch him; one paw was slightly lifted. His whole body quivered. He was like a taut spring, all his being concentrated in his eyes. They were saying as plainly as if he could speak, 'I am yours, if you want me.'

For a long moment Jean-Louis hesitated. He thrust his hands in his pockets and scuffed his sandals in the dust. He was tempted. Throughout his boyhood he had had a dog. There is no better companion on a walking tour than a dog. But there were difficulties. He knew himself all too well. He knew that, once committed, he would never be able to leave this one behind when he went home. France did not have quarantine restrictions. There was nothing to prevent him taking a dog, except for the possible consequences at the other end. He shared his lodgings with another student. He foresaw objections from Henri and

from their landlady. She had never actually forbidden
them to keep a pet. She herself had a cat. Ah! That might
be a problem. All these thoughts were running through
his mind. At last he sighed and shook his head and laughed.
He called '*Pepito!*' and at once the little dog bounded
towards him and rubbed against his legs, whining with
joy.

5

For the next few weeks Pepito lived in a state of continuous bliss. His happiness was so great that at times it was too much to contain. Anyone who had only known the aloof little dog at the Bar Toro would have thought he had suddenly gone crazy. He whirled round and round chasing his tail, rolled, kicked and barked at nothing. In the midst of these antics he would dash up to Jean-Louis and lick his toes or his hand if he could reach it.

Jean-Louis had no fixed itinerary, he went where the fancy took him, avoiding main roads and following dusty tracks to remote villages and wild areas of forest and heath. Whenever possible he spent the night at a hostel or in a monastery where guests were accommodated. In the wilder places he slept in his bedroll under the stars. Always Pepito was at his heels. When they stopped to rest and eat Pepito sat beside him and shared what he had. Up in the mountains it was cold at night and in the small hours when the air was chilliest Pepito would creep into the sleeping bag and fit himself into the curve of his master's body, so that they kept each other warm.

Some days they covered long distances, at other times only a few kilometres. Sometimes the tracks led through lonely farms or vineyards guarded by watchdogs. These dogs were mostly tethered. All they could do was bark at intruders. But some were free and they could be dangerous. It was generally the intrusion of other dogs that they resented, so they chased Pepito rather than Jean-Louis. Pepito prudently ran away from the big ones. In spite of his short legs he could run very fast and easily outdistance them. He stood up to the small ones and gave as good as he got.

The travellers had developed a plan of action that worked well. When they approached one of the lonely farms Jean-Louis would send Pepito on ahead. If a dog came out after him they would avoid the place by taking a roundabout route. If nothing happened but a lot of noisy barking they knew the dog was tied up and they could safely proceed.

It was astonishing how quickly Pepito learnt to play his part. But there was one occasion when he made a bad mistake. They had had to pass through a yard in which they could see, from a distance, a large brown dog standing outside a barn. Pepito had trotted ahead through the gateway, stopped and looked at it. The dog, which was female, had looked back at him and wagged its tail. Pepito, assuming it to be friendly, had sat down and waited for Jean-Louis to follow. Immediately the young man had entered the yard the dog had snarled, hurled itself at him and sunk its teeth in his leg. The tough fabric of his jeans had prevented a more serious injury. The teeth had done little more than break the skin. The dog hung on grimly while Jean-Louis hit it with the stick he always carried and Pepito snapped at its legs. The uproar of shouts, barks and yells had drawn the farmer from his barn. He had called off the dog and apologized for the assault.

'I used to keep her tied up, but not long ago some

gipsies stole my mules and it was only by good luck that I recovered them. Since then I leave her loose.'

'You do well,' Jean-Louis had said ruefully. 'She is an excellent guard.'

'I am very sorry that she hurt you.'

'She was only doing her duty. Do not punish her.'

They had all gone into the house where the farmer had washed the blood off Jean-Louis's leg and put some bright red disinfectant on the wound. They had drunk a glass of wine together and parted good friends.

'Go through the orchard, señor. You will pass a pear tree laden with fruit. Take as many as you want. There are too many pears this year. The price is so low they are not worth picking for the market.'

They had gone on their way – Jean-Louis with a pocketful of pears, Pepito with a mutton bone he had appropriated, neither of them much the worse for the encounter.

The weather was still very hot. Pastures were burnt brown. Streams were often dried up. One that they had to cross, however, still ran strongly. There was no bridge, only stepping stones. Jean-Louis crossed cautiously for the stones were slimy with waterweed. Pepito made a series of careless jumps, slipped and fell in. It was the first time he had been in deep water. He paddled about madly, yelping with fright.

'You see what comes of showing off,' Jean-Louis said, laughing, as he pulled him out. But Pepito was not chastened for very long. He soon recovered his spirits, and on they went. When they came to a specially inviting place they stayed there, idling away the hours beside a running stream or a shining pool. They were both very fit. Pepito's frame had filled out; his coat was sleek and smooth and his muscles had hardened with so much exercise. On their idle days, while Jean-Louis lay and daydreamed, Pepito went lizard hunting. His legs were so short that it was hard for him to see where he was going in rough country, so he tucked them under him and bounced like a rabbit over the rocks and tussocks, making Jean-Louis roar with laughter to watch him. After much practice he became expert at catching lizards and would bring them back in triumph, until he learned that Jean-Louis did not like him to kill them. After that, though he chased them for fun he never hurt them.

There was a bit of the clown in Pepito. He liked to make Jean-Louis laugh and had several ways of doing it. One was to sit with his head cocked on one side, one ear up and the other down. He knew the effect was comical and frequently made use of it. For Jean-Louis was not always gay. He sometimes had fits of melancholy. From the start he had formed the habit of talking to the little dog as they went along, generally of happy or nonsensical things; but sometimes, in the very midst of a bit of nonsense, he would break off and fall silent for an hour or two and the expression on his face would be very sad.

This happened once when they had stopped for a rest beside a lake. It was a lonely place. There was no one about, and no sound but that of a leaping fish. Pepito, sensing his master's change of mood, had come to lick his hand and look inquiringly into his face. Jean-Louis had drawn him close. He had said nothing but stared out over the water, giving a heavy sigh. At last he spoke.

'You want to know what's the matter with me, don't you? Well, I'll tell you. You won't understand but – oh, I don't know, perhaps you will. There's not much you don't know, you clever little cuss. Here it is, then.' And he told Pepito about the girl he loved. She was a fellow student at the law school. They had quarrelled a week before he left for Spain.

'I wanted her to come with me. It's good to have a companion on a trip like this. I planned it all down to the last detail – and then she wouldn't come, for reasons that I was not prepared to accept. I was in the wrong and I knew it, but I couldn't give in. I was proud, you see, like you. Perhaps pride is not a good thing. Perhaps it is better to be humble. If you had been humble, Pepito, you might have been adopted sooner. Ah, but then we wouldn't be together now, would we? So it has worked out all right. You have a master and I a companion. But what am I going to do about Chantal? That's her name. Isn't it pretty? She's pretty, too, and kind and gentle and sweet. You'll love her. But now you must help me to heal this stupid quarrel. Tomorrow we shall be in Pamplona. There I can write her a letter or I can telephone her. What shall I do? Advise me. Shall I phone, and risk a snub?'

Pepito, of course, had not understood a word of all this, but he had felt that some kind of response was expected of him, and so he had barked. At once Jean-Louis had hugged him. 'All right, I will!'

The next day as soon as they reached the town he went to a telephone kiosk and when he came out he looked happy again. 'Your advice was absolutely sound, Pepito.

56

In future I shall take no decisions without consulting you. We have *both* apologized, and all's well between us.' He had bought a packet of sweet biscuits to celebrate the occasion and they had shared them as they made their way through the town to the hostel where they were to stay that night. Jean-Louis couldn't stop talking. 'She sends you her love, Pepito, and looks forward to meeting you. I expect she will ask what made me choose you, for certainly you are no beauty. Then I shall say, "I didn't choose him. He chose *me*." How will you like living in Paris, I wonder? Well, there's a park nearby, but no lizards, I'm afraid.'

The next town they came to was called San Agustin. It was only a small place, with picturesque old buildings, surrounded by high pine-clad hills. It was lunchtime when they reached it, having walked a long way that morning, and Jean-Louis was very hungry. In the main square he found a small restaurant that did not look too expensive and he went in and sat at a table at the back of the room. Those in the front, near the window, were all taken. It was very hot at the back, near the kitchen, and after dropping his pack Jean-Louis took off the light jacket he was wearing and hung it on the loaded coat rack nearby. Pepito sat in his customary place under the table. Having ordered hamburger steak, enough for himself and Pepito, with chip potatoes – to which they were both extremely partial – a green salad and a demi-carafe of wine, Jean-Louis leaned back and waited expectantly for his meal. The restaurant was very busy and seemed to be popular with tourists. He had to wait some time to be served, but when his order came it proved to be worth waiting for.

The meat was well cooked and the salad excellent. Finishing with some fruit, coffee and a cigarette, Jean-Louis felt well satisfied. He fed Pepito and asked for his bill. When it came, he rose to fetch his jacket, in the pocket of which was the wallet that held his money. People were still coming in and out, and other coats had been piled on the rack, which stood in a dark corner. He had to fumble among them to find his own. He paid his bill, added a generous tip for the waiter and when he was ready he walked out, with Pepito close at his heels.

They had only gone a short way down the street and Jean-Louis was waiting for a chance to cross the road when he heard shouts and the sound of running feet somewhere behind him. He swung round and saw the waiter from the restaurant, followed by another man, a big burly fellow with a red face, coming towards him and pointing. 'That's him! That's the one.'

The next moment Jean-Louis was grasped by both arms and held in an iron grip while his assailants went on shouting at him. He was too shocked and bewildered to say anything, or even to struggle. A policeman in the uniform of the civil guard appeared out of nowhere, demanding, 'What's this? What's going on?' Both men began talking at once, very loudly. It was impossible to understand what either of them was saying. The policeman held up his hand. 'One at a time. You –' he commanded the waiter, 'explain what happened. You –' to the other man, 'keep quiet!'

A little knot of spectators had gathered round by now, eagerly listening. 'He took it. I saw him.' 'Took what?'

'The note. The thousand peseta note that is missing from this gentleman's pocket.'

'When I went to get my coat off the rack,' said the red-faced man, 'I found the note was gone.'

'And you say this young man stole it?'

'The waiter says he did.'

'That's right. I saw him,' said the waiter.

The policeman scratched his chin. 'Well, at least he didn't get very far. Would you object to being searched, young man?'

Jean-Louis hesitated. He knew that he had in his wallet a thousand peseta note. It was the last of his holiday money. He also knew that if he objected it would be taken as a sign of his guilt. So he agreed, and all four of them went off to the civil guard quarters near the town hall. Here the search took place and, inevitably, the wallet was examined and the note was revealed.

'There you are,' shouted the red-faced man. 'He's the thief. Arrest him!' It was in vain for Jean-Louis to try and explain that the money was his own. He spoke little Spanish and in his agitation could not make use of the few words and phrases he knew. The result was that he was escorted to an inner office and questioned by the officer in charge. The waiter and the customer who had been robbed were still shouting accusations, some of the onlookers had followed them in from the street, and the place was in an uproar. Pepito, striving to stay close to Jean-Louis, got trampled underfoot and yelped with pain. Nobody took any notice of him, not even Jean-Louis who, in his shocked state, had for the moment forgotten all about him.

The officer had been newly promoted and was at a loss to know what to do in a case like this. San Agustin was only a small town with few facilities for dealing with crime. It did not even have a gaol. The accused was a foreigner, which made it even more awkward. He decided to telephone his superior for instructions. The reply was prompt and decisive. The accused was to be brought for further questioning to police headquarters in the city. Some discussion followed as to whether he was to go by road or rail. Finally it was settled that he would go by road.

And so it happened that within an hour of leaving the restaurant Jean-Louis was pushed into a police car under arrest. Pepito, frantic, tried to jump in after him and was

beaten off with kicks and blows. When the car started he ran after it, his short legs scudding over the tarmac, yelping and crying. Around two sides of the square and down the highway, dodging between other cars, carts and buses, he pelted, falling farther and farther behind until the police car was out of sight. And still he ran on, beyond the boundaries of the town and far out into the country, until at last he dropped exhausted, and lay in the road as if dead.

6

Two little girls found Pepito when they were returning from school that afternoon. He was lying by the roadside and from a distance appeared to be dead. When they drew nearer they saw that he was breathing in short gasps. His mouth was open, his eyes closed. They thought he might have been run over, but there was no mark of injury on his body. When one of them picked him up he seemed to recover from his half-conscious condition. He opened his eyes and feebly wagged his tail.

'What shall we do with him, poor little thing?'

'I don't know.'

'Let's take him home.'

'Mama won't let us keep him. She hates dogs.'

'I know she does. But at least she'll know what to do.'

The place where they lived was not far away and Pepito was so small and light that he was easy to carry. Maria Martinez, the little girl's mother, was a widow who had a small house in the foothills on the outskirts of the town. She was a big, thickset woman with a loud voice, not unkind, but strict with her children. Directly she saw Pepito she said, 'Don't bring it in here. Put it in the woodshed.'

'But, Mama –'

'Do as I say. I won't have dogs in my house. Nasty smelly things, full of fleas. Where did you find it?'

'In the road. He isn't hurt, but he seems to be ill.'

'Put it in the shed. See that it has some water to drink. Tomorrow I'll tell Paco to come and fetch it.'

'Oh no, Mama!'

'Don't argue. It's the only thing to do.'

Paco Morales, the dog-catcher of San Agustin, was an old soldier with a lame leg and a patch over one eye. He had accepted the post because, with his disabilities, it was all he could get. It was a far cry from fighting insurgents in Morocco to impounding stray dogs in this peaceful little town, but he accepted it, as he did most things in this life, philosophically, and he made the best of it.

The pound was a big dark barn smelling of the goats which had formerly been housed in it. Along the walls were ring bolts to which the dogs were tied at safe distances from each other. This prevented them from fighting for, like all prisoners, they were quarrelsome and unhappy. They were mostly mongrels. The handsomer ones had either strayed from their homes or run away because they were not well treated. The majority were street dogs adopted by holiday-makers and then abandoned when the holiday-makers left without making provision for them. These were often starving when brought in.

There were ten dogs in the pound at this time, of all kinds and temperaments. Many were small and docile, but there were some who were big and vicious. The dog-catcher was often afraid when he had to deal with dogs like these, but he had to capture them or lose his job, and he did it as best he could so that neither he nor they got hurt in the process. His equipment was a stout pole with a hinged iron hoop on the end of it. The method was to get as near as possible to his quarry by talking kindly to it, or offering a biscuit, and then to clap the hoop about its neck. It was then helpless, no matter how hard it struggled and snapped. Some did not struggle at all but went willingly, grateful for some human attention. The windows of the pound had recently had bars fitted to them. This was because attempts were made from time to time to set the captives free. The dog-catcher was not liked by local children, who were sorry for the dogs. When they found a stray they would hide it until the dog-catcher had passed. It was no good telling them that animals running loose can cause traffic accidents, or that a homeless dog – which cannot fend for itself like a cat – is often better dead.

What with capturing the dogs, feeding and watering them, ridding them of ticks and fleas, keeping his records and making up his accounts, Paco was a busy man with little time to stop and chat. He therefore pretended not to see his cousin Maria Martinez while he was hurrying back from the butcher's that sunny morning. But Maria had spotted him. She ran after him, calling, 'Paco! Hey, Paco, stop! I've got something to tell you.' It would have been useless to pretend that he hadn't heard. Maria's voice carried even over the noise of the cement mixer on the building site opposite. Paco was obliged to stop. 'Be quick then,' he said.

'It's about a dog,' Maria panted. 'My girls brought it home yesterday. No clue to the owner. You'd better come and fetch it.'

'All right. I'll try to come tonight.' Paco hurried on his way with his sackful of bones and scraps.

64

Back in the pound he distributed the food among various old tin cans which served the inmates as plates, and re-filled the drinking bowls. Most of the dogs reacted pleasurably to these attentions; but there was one whose only response was to give a menacing growl every time the dog-catcher went near him. This was a big Alsatian – a *cane lupo*, or wolf dog, as the Spaniards call this breed – who had been caught a week ago. No one knew where he had come from. The name plate was missing from his shabby old collar. He was in good condition but no longer young. There were rusty grey streaks in his fur and scars on his muzzle. It would be a long time before Paco would forget how the big dog had fought him every inch of the way as he was dragged off to the pound. Despite the leather gauntlets, which were all the protection he had against what he called 'unwilling guests', the dog-catcher's jacket was torn, his hands were bruised and his arms ached for days after the struggle. Once secured, however, the Alsatian had quietened down and given no trouble. But he always snarled when approached. Paco called him Lupo, for lack of any other name. It suited him well.

Tied up next to him was a young hunting dog of the native breed. He looked as though he had never had enough to eat and his bony form contrasted sharply with those of the over-fed pets who were waiting to be re-claimed, and who turned up their noses at the rough fare provided for them here. The young hound had been the weakling of a litter born on a farm and reared for rabbit hunting. He had the build of a greyhound but owing to some defect in his muscles he was useless for hunting. His master could neither sell him nor give him away, but could not bring himself to shoot him. So he took him to a rubbish dump on the far side of the town, tied him to a tree and left him for the dog-catcher to take. Paco named him 'Guapo', which means handsome, in mockery of the poor creature's ugliness.

When he had finished his work in the barn Paco went home to lunch. After he had eaten and had a siesta he set out for Maria's cottage, which was some distance away. He went on foot instead of on his motorcycle because, having omitted in his haste to ask for further details, he didn't know what sort of a dog Maria's daughters had found. If it was a big one, or even medium size, he would have to lead it on a rope.

As it turned out, he did not collect it at all, for when he reached the cottage the girls came running out to tell him the dog was gone. It was the fault of Manolo, their brother, who had been sent to fetch wood for the fire and cautioned not to let the dog out – but as usual had been careless. The dog had dodged past him when he opened the door, and vanished into the trees behind the villa.

'He should have opened the door just a *little* way and *peeped* in,' said Juana. 'But he pulled it wide.'

'He is so stupid,' said Pilar. 'He does everything wrong. But we are glad the dog escaped. It was a dear little thing. We would have liked to keep it, but Mama wouldn't let us.'

Paco went off grumbling, having had the long walk there and back for nothing.

The hill behind the cottage was densely covered with pine trees, one of which had blown down in a gale leaving a shallow pit where the roots had torn out. In this pit lay

Pepito, his heart still pounding painfully after his uphill flight. His strength had been tried to the limit when he chased the police car so far the day before. But worse than the physical weakness was his mental distress.

Only twenty-four hours ago he had been a confident exuberant little animal, secure in the love and possession of his master and without a care. Now his world had collapsed about him. He had no idea how he came to be lying here in the hollow. His memory stopped short at the terrible moment when the car drove off, taking Jean-Louis away from him. The compulsion to search for his beloved friend was urgent, but first he had to rest, to be strong again. He curled up, wedging himself deeper into the loose earth, and slept until daylight faded. Then he was wakened by the onset of a late summer storm. Distant thunder cracked over the hills and rain began to fall. It washed the dust and earth off him and trickled in rivulets down the sides of the hollow. He got up, feeling stiff and cold, and set out to find some shelter among the rocks and gullies of the hillside.

When Paco returned to the pound he was tired and limping badly. It was probably on this account that he forgot to close the padlock on the door before he went home. Two boys from the town noticed this as they were passing by later that night. They whispered together and giggled, then stealthily opened the door and went in.

The dogs were asleep, but the rattle of the chain and scrape of the heavy door wakened them and they lifted their heads in eager interest. It was a fine night, after the rain, and there was enough light to see by. But it was not so easy to release the dogs as the boys had expected. Constant tugging and straining had knotted the ropes too tightly, and as the boys had entered the barn on impulse they had not brought a knife with which to cut them. Guapo was easy to free because he had hardly struggled at all. They were afraid to go near Lupo who looked too fierce. But Lupo, as it happened, freed himself. He was so big and heavy that he had frayed his rope by straining against it; and now, when he lunged at the boys, it snapped. Thoroughly scared, they dashed to the door, leaving it open, and pelted off as fast as they could.

The two dogs, at first, did not run anywhere. They hung about, undecided on what to do. Then Lupo came to a decision and trotted off without looking back. Guapo immediately followed him. They took a footpath that avoided the town and led up into the hills that stretched for miles in all directions. It was ideal country for fugitives, as Lupo knew well. In a cave in those hills he had lived for a long time, so cunningly that no one suspected he was there or even knew that he was still alive. It was supposed by his late owners that he had met with an accident after he ran away. It was only by pure chance that he had been caught by the dog-catcher on one of his stealthy excursions into the town in search of food.

Free again now, through some strange intervention of fate, he lost no time in making for his old refuge. He moved fast, behind him the thin hound whose spindly legs stumbled and sprawled over the tree roots on the stony track.

The track led through the ravine, a deep cleft in the hillside filled with great boulders that had tumbled down from the summit in some ancient upheaval. Hidden among them was the mouth of the cave which had been home to Lupo for so long before he was captured. He could have found his way to it on the blackest night by scent alone. Eagerly he ran towards it but, when still some distance away, he suddenly stopped, lifted his muzzle and growled. He had picked up the scent of another dog. Guapo stopped too when he caught up, sensing that something was wrong. After a pause Lupo went on with slow and wary steps. Nearing the cave he crouched and growled again deep in his throat. Framed in the starlit entrance, facing him, was the black-and-white head of a small shaggy dog. The two of them stared at each other for a long moment, motionless. They might have been carved out of stone.

Pepito was frightened, and his eyes showed it. But he stood his ground and gradually the tension slackened. Lupo's gaze wavered. Guapo closed up behind him, whining and sniffing. Tails began to wag, cautiously at first, then with more confidence. Pepito gave a friendly yap. Lupo answered with a short bark. Then all three of them trotted round investigating every nook and cranny of the cave.

Pepito was accepted by the other two but his nature inclined him to keep a little apart, as it had always done since the days of his puppyhood, whereas Guapo kept close to Lupo. Had these two been able to exchange confidences as humans do they would have found much in common. Both had suffered at the hands of men. The Alsatian had not been actively ill-treated like Guapo but had been ill-used in a different way. He had been the guard dog at a warehouse, chained up all day and released at night to patrol the concrete yard behind the barrier. He had no company. Food was brought to him twice a day, but no one ever came to talk to him or take him for a run. He became morose and unapproachable. The sight of green grass and the smell of fresh earth outside the enclosure tormented him until he was frantic to get out. He began to practise leaping up against the high wire fence, gradually going higher and higher until one night, with a tremendous leap, he cleared it and dropped down on the other side, free to go where he pleased. At once he had made for the hills and after wandering for a time had found this cave. He had spent the summer lying up by day and slipping out at night to forage for food in the town. Several of the hotels and restaurants had pig bins into which all the table scraps were thrown at the end of the day, ready to be collected by the farmers who drove in early in the mornings bringing their produce to market. The bins were put out at night for the sake of coolness, otherwise the contents would have gone bad. Meat, bones, sometimes whole chicken carcasses, were thrown in. Lupo had quickly learned how to lift the lids off the bins and never had any difficulty in getting as much as he wanted, and what he took was never missed. It had been while foraging in the alley near the kitchen entrance of the Hotel Flores that he had been caught. He was far too clever to be taken in the same way a second time. But as it turned out later, his cleverness in this respect was not to be put to the test.

In the city gaol a hundred kilometres away Jean-Louis lay on a wooden bench that served for a bed. The dirty walls of the cell, the hardness of the bench, the stale air and intermittent noises of clanging gates and tramping feet, all combined to induce a feeling of being in a kind of waking nightmare. He still could not entirely believe that it was really happening to him, that he was here in this horrible place and likely to remain here for some time – unless a miracle intervened to get him out of it.

On arrival he had been stripped, all his possessions had been taken away and he had been subjected to long and detailed questioning. He answered as well as he could in his bad Spanish, protesting his innocence over and over again. The police were not harsh or intimidating. On the contrary, they even seemed to want to help him. He had the impression that he was something of an embarrassment and that they didn't really know, or else couldn't make up their minds, what to do with him.

'Can you produce an alibi?' asked one of the officers.

'No, of course not. I was in the restaurant at the time of the theft and many people saw me. I am not a liar, or a thief.' Finally they told him that they were awaiting instructions. In the meantime, at his own request, they had contacted the French Honorary Consul in Pamplona. When this gentleman arrived he had a long talk with Jean-Louis. 'It seems that you have not yet been charged. The decision rests with the Procurator.'

'Can you help me?' asked Jean-Louis.

'My powers are limited but I will do what I can.'

'The most urgent thing,' said Jean-Louis, 'is to get through to my parents in Rouen and ask them to send me some money. I shall need a lawyer.'

'I doubt if it will come to that. The amount of money

you are alleged to have stolen is too small, in my opinion, to warrant the cost of a trial. But most certainly your parents should be told of your predicament.'

'What do you think will happen to me?'

'I imagine that when they have finished arguing they will decide to deport you as an – er, undesirable character.'

Jean-Louis flushed. It was true that his appearance was against him. His hair was rather long, his jeans were faded and stained and his sandals were worn through the soles. 'One doesn't wear a smart suit to go tramping the mountains of Spain,' he said. 'I am not a vagabond but a law student in my third year of studies. And I object to being sent out of the country with this stain on my character. I demand a trial and a chance of proving that I am not a thief. Will you tell them that?'

'Very well. I'll talk to the Chief when I get a chance, and put your point of view. It's all most unfortunate. Is there anything else?'

'Yes, I had a dog, a small terrier. I'm very anxious about him. He was with me when I was arrested and driven away. He tried to get into the car. I last saw him running behind it. Would you telephone the police in San Agustin and ask if they have found him?'

'I'll do so right away and let you know what they say.'

'I'm most grateful.'

When the Consul returned he shook his head and said, 'I'm sorry not to have better news. No one knows what became of the dog. It was last seen chasing the car, as you said. After that – it just seems to have disappeared.'

7

The next morning, when the dog-catcher went to the pound, he was horrified to find the door ajar and two dogs missing. He remembered then that he had neglected to snap the padlock when he left on the previous evening, and his state of mind was not helped by the reflection that what had occurred was entirely his own fault. In the absence of any human culprit on whom to vent his wrath he took it out on his charges, hitting one with the broom handle when she got in his way and kicking another that upset the drinking bowl. He hurt his lame leg more than he hurt them, and this added to his sense of injury.

To make matters worse, when he was in the midst of his morning tasks, in walked his neighbour Señora Carrera, the local busybody. After watching him for a few minutes she asked, 'What's the matter? Why are you looking so bad-tempered?'

Paco would have liked to ignore her, but he knew it was useless. 'Because some miscreant broke in here during the night and let out two of the dogs, that's why.'

'Who on earth could it have been? Dog thieves?'

'Rubbish. Just some silly kids having a lark, I expect.'

'Yes, but –'

'Do you mind getting out of my way? I have to sweep the floor.'

Señora Carrera did not move. 'How do you think they got in?'

'Forced the lock, I dare say. It wouldn't be difficult.'

'How do you know they weren't dog thieves?'

'Because the missing ones are of no value.'

'What about the wolf dog? I see he's gone.'

She had a point there. The big Alsatian, though old, was certainly a valuable animal and it was possible an owner might turn up to claim it. There was also the unfortunate fact that Señora Carrera was a gossip as well as a busybody and it would soon be common knowledge that some dogs had escaped from the pound. If it reached the ears of the Mayor there might be an inquiry. The town council of San Agustin had recently elected a new mayor, a very different character from his affable easygoing predecessor. Everyone regretted Don Rodrigo's retirement. Don Anselmo was the type to order an inquiry into the smallest irregularity and ask a great many awkward questions. It was a worried man who swept the floor of the pound and spread clean straw that morning.

Directly he had finished Paco put on his leather gauntlets and went out to see if he could find the tracks of the runaways. It had rained in the night, which was lucky for him. The tracks were visible, sure enough, and they led in the expected direction, towards the foothills on the outskirts of the town. He could not follow them for more than a few hundred yards for the soft ground ended at the tarmac road. So he went back for his motorcycle, mounted it and set off. Branching from the main highway was a side road leading to a farm at the foot of the hills where the woods began. Here he left the motorcycle and took the narrow footpaths used by hunters and charcoal burners. He knew them well, for on fiestas he liked to borrow a gun and go rabbit shooting with his friends. He had been right in guessing that this was the area the missing dogs would make for. But he did not know about the cave.

All that day the dogs lay dozing and waiting for nightfall. Two of them at least did not understand why they had to wait for darkness before they could venture out. They only knew that every time they tried to do so their leader snarled angrily. Lupo had established complete authority and no move could be made without his permission. Pepito was unhappy, torn between the desire to stay with his new friends and the compulsion to go in search of Jean-Louis. He was restless and whimpered in his sleep.

The day passed slowly. Night fell and the moon rose, but even then Lupo would allow no move. Not until the moon had set and there was no light but that of the stars, in the absolute hush of the hour before dawn, Lupo led his companions out of the cave and down the ravine, making a detour round the farm so as not to alert the guard dog, and emerging finally at the junction of the lane with the main road. He moved with extreme care and skill, halting at the slightest sound. The others were less skilful. When Guapo blundered Lupo did not punish him. He seemed to know that Guapo's clumsiness was something he could not help.

Silent as shadows, slipping from cover to cover, the three of them entered the sleeping town. Lupo had automatically reverted to his old routine. But many things had changed in San Agustin with the election of the new Mayor. Don Anselmo was a new broom who intended to sweep clean. He wanted tourists to be impressed by the tidiness of the streets, so he had decreed that food bins were no longer to be left out at night. They could be put out first thing in the morning for the farmers and if the contents had spoiled then the garbage collectors would remove it. Naturally it did spoil when the weather was hot and the farmers grumbled loudly. But Don Anselmo had good reason for making the new rule. Though stray dogs were now dealt with by the dog-catcher there were numbers of homeless cats who raided the bins, often upsetting them and littering the streets, thus attracting rats and other vermin. Hygiene was a modern necessity which had to be considered if the town were to develop as a tourist resort.

The regulation had come into force during Lupo's captivity in the pound, so of course he knew nothing about it. He was puzzled to find the pig bin missing from its accustomed place outside the kitchen entrance of the Hotel Flores, but not really alarmed. There were other hotels and other bins. He trotted off and the others followed him from place to place, from street to street, with Pepito always in the rear looking smaller than ever by comparison with his two companions. All the rest of that night they prowled about the town, nowhere finding anything to eat. When dawn came they went back to the cave to sleep.

Paco Morales returned to his house after a fruitless search of the pine woods feeling very dejected. His lame leg was hurting badly after all that scrambling over rocks and tree roots. He was too tired to eat any supper. All he wanted to do was to go to bed. He was on the point of doing so when there was a thunderous knock on the door and in burst Marta, his neighbour.

'I heard there's been a break-in at the pound and all the dogs have escaped!'

Paco smiled sourly. 'Then you heard wrong. *Two* are missing, that's all.'

'Who let them out?'

'How should I know? Kids getting up to mischief.'

'I don't see how they could do it,' Marta said.

'Well, they did,' Paco snapped, sticking to his story. 'They got in and let loose *two* of the dogs, who may be miles away by now – and if they are they can stay there. They aren't bothering me or anyone else and I'm not going to wear myself out tramping the country in search of them. Now, if you don't mind, I'm going to bed. Good*night*.'

The next day it was not so easy for Lupo to keep control in the cave. Hunger made the other inmates restive and disobedient. They kept trying to slip out. Each time Lupo drove them back. But he knew that he could not hold them much longer and at last he let them go. Noisy and careless, they bounded out and were soon lost among the trees. There were rabbit tracks to follow and these were exciting but unrewarding. The exercise made them hungrier, but they caught nothing except a few lizards which only Guapo would eat and a fieldmouse which made less than a mouthful for Lupo who had now joined them.

The noise they made was heard by Maria who was hanging out her washing. She dropped her basket of pegs, flung on a shawl and caught the bus into town to tell Paco. 'They're up on the hill. I heard them. Come quickly!'

'All right, all right. Not so fast. What exactly did you hear?'

'The racket dogs make when they are chasing something. Yelping. Barking.'

'What sort of barking?'

'Loud and deep. Coming from big dogs, for sure. But there was also some yapping. It looks as if that little black-and-white one is with them.'

'Could be. You might put out some food and see if you can catch him for me.'

'What about the others? That wolf dog could be dangerous. I don't want to think of my children playing in the woods with an animal like that at large.'

'Keep them at home then.'

'You know perfectly well I can't do that. Anyway it's your job to deal with matters of this kind. You're the dog-catcher.'

'It's not my job to go chasing about the countryside after runaways.'

'There'll be trouble if you don't. You'll see.'

Paco knew that Maria was right. He would have to make another attempt to capture the missing animals. Two of them were hunting dogs and therefore potential killers. If anything bad should happen he would be sure to get the blame. 'All right,' he said. 'I'll come.'

During the next few days, with Maria and her children helping, he made a thorough search of the hillside, to no avail. The fugitives lay quiet in their hide-out, venturing out only when it was safe to look for food. They found nothing and by the fourth day of their freedom were weak from hunger. Guapo's legs shook so badly that he could hardly stand. He could not take more than a few steps without falling down, and sometimes it seemed as if he would never get up again. Pepito's ribs were showing again and he whimpered miserably in the corner of the cave he had made his own.

One morning, quite early, Lupo rose and went off alone without waking the others. Hunting in broad day-light was risky, but Lupo was beyond caution. He took the path that led round the foot of the hill to join the tarmac road. There was a lot of traffic on it so he crouched in a ditch waiting for a chance to cross. On the other side were several holiday villas which, though it was late in the season, were still occupied. Where there were people there was often food to be had. Lupo's fear of human contact now took second place to his hunger. But his present objective was not the holiday houses. He was making for a small farm a short way up the road with some mixed livestock, sheep, goats and chickens, all running loose to-gether in an enclosure bounded by wire netting. Lupo knew that he could leap over the barrier easily. But he had to make his raid in the daytime. At night all the livestock were shut up in pens with heavy doors and no windows.

There was still too much traffic so he crept along in the ditch till he reached a point right opposite the little farm. Here he lay, awaiting his opportunity to rush the fence. His amber eyes were fixed on the fat hens that pecked and scratched contentedly among the rubbish in the enclosure. For a dog of his size and strength it would be no great feat to jump out again with a hen in his mouth. But first he had to cross the road without being seen. It was the busiest time of the day and there were cars and vans going both ways. The noise was torture to Lupo's sensitive ears; but loud as it was, he suddenly heard above it a cry from across the road. A lamb had got out through a hole in the netting and its mother was anxiously calling it. The little creature had forgotten the way back and was running round, bleating plaintively. The ground fell away sharply between the fence and the road, and as Lupo watched, the lamb's wobbling legs stumbled and it slid down the bank into the road, right in the path of an oncoming car. There was a squeal of brakes. The car jolted to a stop. A man got out and went to the front of it. He seemed upset at what he saw and stood for a moment scratching his head as if he did not know what to do. He looked at the farmhouse, but there was no one there who could have seen the accident. He looked at his watch, and then appeared to come to a decision. After waiting for a lull in the traffic he bent down, dragged the dead lamb from under the bumper, carried it across the road and dropped it in the ditch. Then he returned to the car and drove rapidly away.

The lamb lay only a few yards from Lupo. His mouth watered as he looked at it and saliva dripped from his tongue. He did not hesitate for long but seized the lamb, pulled it into deeper cover in a clump of bamboos and began to tear ravenously at the warm flesh. When his hunger was satisfied he lay down and rested, but he did not sleep. He was trying to resolve the conflict in his

prompted him to bury the rest of the meat and return to it later. But at the same time he wanted to take his prize back to his friends. He lay in the bamboo clump for some while longer, torn by indecision. Finally loyalty swayed him. He rose, took a firm grip of the carcase and began to drag it over the stony track to the ravine, and thence to the cave.

The lamb was missed that evening when the old woman to whom it belonged went to water her flock. Her animals often broke out and it was surprising that more of them were not run over. It seemed likely that the missing lamb had met this fate. But she could not understand why there were no marks of the accident to be seen, despite her careful search of the roadway. An animal hit by a car usually dies of shock and its body lies where it falls. No one would take it for fear of being thought responsible for its death. News of the missing lamb spread quickly among her neighbours but nobody could account for it. It might well have remained a mystery but for the sharp eyes of Manolo Martinez.

It was a school half-holiday and Manolo was out hunting sparrows with his airgun when he noticed a tuft of white wool snagged on a bramble bush on the hill track above the cottage. A little further on he saw another, and then some drops of blood on the ground. This was exciting. Creeping like an Indian on the warpath he followed the trail until he reached the ravine. Here there was more blood – a pool of it on a boulder – still fresh, for the sun did not penetrate the ravine. For this reason children tended to avoid it, like all dark and silent places.

Manolo, however, spurred on by excitement and curiosity, squirmed through the tumbled rocks until, to his astonishment, he found himself looking into the mouth of a large cave. Although he lived so near, he had never suspected its existence. In the dark interior he could make out the shapes of some animals lying close together. They were dogs, apparently fast asleep. Beside them was something he could not at first identify. When his eyes adjusted he recognized it as the mangled remains of a lamb.

Manolo drew a deep breath. Slight as it was, the sound wakened two of the dogs. The bigger one sprang up and snarled ferociously, standing guard over the other. Manolo beat a hasty retreat. He scrambled down the hill to tell his mother. Maria hurried out to the farm to tell the old woman, and the old women told her neighbours.

That evening a deputation went to the town hall to talk to the Mayor. The Mayor lost no time in sending for the dog-catcher. He sat in his office behind a huge desk, looking very stern. 'I understand that some dogs have escaped from the pound.'

'That's true, your honour,' said Paco nervously. 'Some scoundrel broke in and –'

'Never mind how it happened. Why haven't you recaptured them?'

'Well, it's not easy. My leg makes it hard for me to get about. I've tried to find them. But I'd like to point out with respect that my job is to keep strays off the streets, not to go chasing about the country –'

'Your job,' Don Anselmo said testily, 'is to deal with strays wherever they may be. This lot, for your information, have begun killing lambs and must be dealt with immediately. The son of Maria Martinez will show you where they are lying up. Find some men to go with you. Waste no time – and shoot at sight.'

'It's too late now, your honour, the light's going –'

'I know that, you fool. Get your posse organized tonight and do the job first thing tomorrow morning, before any more damage is done.'

'Will they shoot them all?' the little girls wanted to know when Maria returned with her news. 'Even the little black-and-white one?'

84

'That is the Mayor's order.'

'But, Mama, he is so small. He couldn't have killed anything.'

Maria was busy cooking the supper. Her feet ached after all that walking and her patience was short. 'Well, I can't help it, can I?'

'We could save him – if we went to the cave tonight.'

Maria swung round with a scraped carrot in her hand and shook it at her children angrily. 'You keep away from that place, do you hear me? What happens to a lot of bad dogs is nothing to do with you.'

'But, Mama –' said Manolo, 'I have to show the men where it is. Without me they'll never find it.'

'All right. You'll lead them there and you'll come straight back before the shooting begins. Understand?'

'Yes, Mama.'

Before nine o'clock next morning Manolo, Paco and his friend Pedro the civil guard, were on their way up the hill. With them were Miguel of the Bar Mañana and Toni, the nephew of the old woman whose lamb had been killed. Pedro had his pistol. The rest carried guns. They followed the boy Manolo up the ravine, their heavy boots ringing and scraping on the rocks.

The dogs heard them coming from a long way off. But there was no way of escape except through the ravine, so they backed into the farthest and darkest corner of the cave and waited there, tense with fear. The noise of the boots and the voices increased and presently the forms of several men appeared in the entrance. One of them produced a torch and swung it round in a wide arc until the beam picked out, right at the back, the crouching shapes and gleaming eyes. 'There they are!'

Four weapons were raised simultaneously. A volley of shots rang out, filling the cave with thunder and the smell of cordite. No more were needed.

8

The sound of the shots, reverberating through the woods, was heard over a wide area. Maria heard it while she was washing up the breakfast things after packing her children off to school. She knew that when the men came down from the hill they would pass fairly near her cottage and, remembering the sad faces of her daughters, she ran to meet them, still in her dressing gown and slippers. 'How many dogs were there?' she asked.

'Two,' said Paco.

'Was one of them a sort of terrier, black and white, not much bigger than a cat?'

'No, no,' said Miguel, pointing to the heavy sacks Pedro and Toni carried. 'They were big, both of them. One was a wolf dog, the other a hound. Real killers, by the look of them.'

'I wonder what happened to the little one,' Maria pondered as she went back to her sink.

What had saved Pepito was a quarrel that took place in the cave on the night before the shooting. He had made the mistake of trying to snatch a mouthful of meat while the others were feeding. At once Lupo turned on him, bit him savagely and drove him out. The little dog's position from the start had been one of subservience. There were limits to what Lupo would tolerate. Even so, it is unlikely that he would have behaved like this in different circumstances. The weather had been extremely hot during the past two days, and the discomfort of this in close and airless confinement, combined with privation, no doubt precipitated the attack.

Pepito made no attempt to defend himself. He fled up the hillside as fast as he could go. Lupo did not pursue him, being too wise to waste energy in such heat. But Pepito ran on and on and did not stop till he had put more than a mile between himself and the cave. The pain in his side where Lupo's teeth had met was hurting badly. A tuft of fur had been torn clean out and the wound was bleeding. He licked it clean and presently, when the pain lessened, settled down to rest.

He slept till the sun was high. But it was not this that wakened him for he was lying in the shade of a tree. It was something else. A distinctive odour had crept stealthily into the hot stillness of the pine woods and mingled with the scents of earth and wild herbs. It was the smell of smoke.

Pepito sat up and wrinkled his nose, not knowing why the smell alarmed him. He stretched, walked a little way, then sat on his haunches. The disturbing smell was coming from the north, from the other side of the hill; and now he could see that the outlines of the trees along the summit were unclear, blurred by a haze rising from below. Growing more and more uneasy, he ran towards them, moving awkwardly because of the stiffness in his hind legs. His side hurt where blood had congealed on the wound during the night. Every now and then he stopped to lick it. In a few minutes he reached the brow of the hill and from here could see through the haze into the valley beyond. It was wild country, the haunt of rabbits and other small game, rough and stony, overgrown with rosemary, juniper and wild thyme. Through the tussocks crept tongues of flame, like scarlet snakes. Tinder-dry, the undergrowth was aflame in a dozen places. Even while Pepito stared, the red tongues ran up to the foot of the hill and touched the first clump of pine trees, leaping like living things up the trunks and into the resinous boughs till, in a moment, each tree burned like a torch. In other parts the same thing was happening. The fire spread with terrible speed, fanned by the wind of its own creation. Flaming twigs flew on ahead to ignite other trees until on all sides the hill was alight. The cracking and splitting of the blazing branches was accompanied by a deafening roar like the roar of the sea in a gale.

Pepito backed away from the sight, so frightened and confused that he did not know which way to turn. So he ran in a halting circle that gradually diminished as the carpet of pine needles caught fire under the showers of sparks blowing on them in the hot wind. Now there was fire underfoot as well as all around him and he was forced to make a dash through it, so terrified that he scarcely felt the pain of his scorched pads. More by luck than intention he fled in the only safe direction. This was a part of the woods frequented by charcoal burners. They had felled the trees and stripped the undergrowth over a large area in the path of the fire. Here Pepito's headlong flight came to an end and here he stayed until the conflagration died down on the edge of the clearing.

The ground here was blackened and bare, marked with

a series of shallow pits around the edges of which were small fragments of charcoal left from the burnings. Piled on end against a roughly made hut were branches ready for use. Between the logs and the wall of the hut was a cavity like a wigwam, offering a welcome patch of shade from the noonday glare. Pepito crept in. But now he could hear other noises, the shouts and yells of firefighters in the valley who were beating out the flames with long-handled brooms made of twigs. The voices drew nearer as the men climbed the hill. They sounded threatening to Pepito, and he decided to leave the shelter. Fright had robbed him of all sense of direction, but once again luck was with him, bringing him back in a wide circle into the vicinity of the Martinez cottage. Directly above it and separated from it by a jungle of matted undergrowth was an old ruined building. It was a chapel, erected many years ago by the grateful family of a man who had recovered, as if by a miracle, from a deadly illness. Long fallen into disuse, the chapel was now a favourite haunt of small boys who liked to hide in it and take pot shots at birds with their airguns.

Pepito pushed through the tangled bushes. Brambles tore at his wound and he was panting with thirst. Reaching the building he stopped to rest and was about to flop down when he suddenly lifted his head and tensed. He had smelt water. His sensitive nose led him quickly to the disused well, but the discovery was useless to him. The well held only a few inches of water at the bottom of the shaft. Pepito jumped on to the crumbling wall and looked in, tormented with longing for the water he could see and smell but could not reach. The wall was in such a bad state that it gave way even under his light weight. With a yelp of terror he pitched forward and down, amid a shower of broken cement and stones, down through rushing air and deepening darkness, down and down . . .

In the gaol where Jean-Louis was awaiting the Procurator's visit there had been a dramatic development. The officer in charge of the civil guard in San Agustin was talking over the telephone to his opposite number at police headquarters in the city. 'In connection with the prisoner Leblanc – we have a lad here who was caught leaving the town in a stolen car. He told a pathetic tale about having to visit his dying grandmother in a village some distance away and having no money for the fare because he had been gambling –'

'Yes, yes, but what has this got to do with Leblanc?'

'I'm coming to that. We checked on his story and found it was untrue. His grandmother turned out to be the healthiest old lady I've met in years. Meanwhile the owner of the car declared that when the vehicle was taken it had very little petrol in the tank. It was restored to him with the tank half full. So how did the thief, who had gambled all his money away, raise enough to buy the petrol? You may well ask. On being interrogated he confessed to picking a pocket at the Marisol Restaurant – yes, that's right, the place where Leblanc was arrested last week. The waiter who denounced him has now admitted that he could have been mistaken. So it's all clear to release Leblanc and let's hope the French Consulate won't make too much fuss about wrongful arrest. It's always tricky when foreigners are picked up for minor offences. But we have to do the best we can. Right. I'll send this lad along as soon as possible, with the papers. What's that? Still on about his dog, is he? No, there's no news of it, so far as I know. It's not been impounded, that's certain. I'll continue to make inquiries, but I don't hold out much hope of finding it after all this time.'

In Maria's kitchen, on the following day, Manolo was eating his breakfast. When he had finished he went upstairs to fetch his cap and satchel. He slept in a tiny room at the back of the cottage facing the hillside. It was time to go to school, but Manolo didn't like school and didn't want to go, so he dawdled about, thrust his head out of the window and listened to the chirping of sparrows in the trees. Suddenly he frowned and his expression changed. He leaned farther out, listening more intently, then drew in his head and ran downstairs to find his sisters. The three of them went outside and listened to the mournful cries that came from somewhere on the hillside. There was a gusty wind blowing and sometimes the cries sounded quite loud, at other times so faint that they could hardly be heard.

'Do you think it's the little one?' asked Juana.

'It might be. Anyway it's an animal in trouble.'

Three heads came together and a plan was made.

Maria watched them stroll off down the lane, suspecting nothing. The minute she had gone back indoors the three children turned and began to scramble up the steep and narrow track that led to the old chapel. The higher they climbed the more clearly they could hear the howling. And when they reached the spot, the broken wall of the well told its own story. Peering in, they saw the little black-and-white dog standing in the water far below, looking up at them with tragic, terrified eyes.

'How are we ever going to get him out?'

'I don't know, unless Mama will help us.'

'I bet she won't.'

'We can ask her. She'll be cross with us, but she just *might* help.'

She certainly was cross when she found they hadn't gone to school. There was a deal of scolding, argument and protestation.

'But we can't leave him there. He'll die!'

And finally she agreed to help, as they had known she would. But on her own conditions. 'You two,' she told the girls, 'go off to school. I'll take Manolo, as he's the strongest, and we'll see what we can do. And *if* we get him out of there, he's to be taken to the pound, understand?'

'But, Mama, what's the use of saving his life and then giving him to the dog-catcher? You know what will happen to him.'

'I don't, and nor do you. His owner might turn up, or someone might offer to adopt him.'

'Why couldn't it be us?'

'I've said no and I mean no. That's enough argument. Off with you.'

In an emergency Maria could be both reliable and re-sourceful. She now rose magnificently to the occasion. She climbed up to the chapel to assess the situation. She looked down the shaft and said grimly to Pepito, 'Oh, it's you again, is it?' Then she tested the iron framework of the well-head to make sure that it was sound enough to bear some weight. She sent Manolo back to the cottage to fetch the bucket and rope from her own well. While he was gone she worked on the pulley, scraping off the flakes of rust with stone chips until it worked fairly smoothly. When Manolo returned with the rope she passed the free end of it over the pulley and dropped the bucket a little way down the shaft. Then she told Manolo to step into it. Manolo blenched. He was only nine years old and not very brave. He looked up at the ancient well-head which was so frail that it shook at every touch. 'What if it breaks, Mama?'

'It won't break. Get in. Keep still and hold on to the rope while I lower you down.'

Knowing that opposition was futile, Manolo stepped into the bucket. The first part of the operation was easy for a woman as strong as Maria. But it was another matter when the bucket had reached the bottom of the well and she had to haul up both boy and dog. The double burden was almost too much. More than once the rope nearly slipped out of her grasp. For Manolo too it was a test of strength as well as courage. On his mother's shouted instructions he had grasped Pepito round the middle and hoisted him over his shoulder so that the front paws hung down his back. This left him one arm free with which to cling to the rope. Pepito did not struggle, either because he was too exhausted or because he understood that they were trying to help him.

It was dark and icy-cold down there. The bucket swung about and bumped against the rough walls of the shaft with a hollow clanking sound. Up above Manolo could see Maria's flushed face and hear her prayers to the saints as she heaved and hauled. Perhaps the prayers helped, for the bucket came up a few inches at a time, sometimes with a jerk, sometimes infinitely slowly, till Manolo was at last able to step out with his burden. His elbows were skinned from rubbing against the rough concrete and he was pale and shaking with fright. Pepito was trembling too. His legs would hardly support him. But he seemed unharmed by his fall. He licked Manolo's face and allowed himself to be hugged and stroked.

'Pleased to see us, aren't you? And no wonder. That was a nasty scrape you got yourself into,' Maria said. After removing her rope from the well-head she tied one end round Pepito's neck. He showed no inclination to run away, but Maria was taking no chances. They returned to the cottage where Maria dressed the grazes on Manolo's arms and then sent him off to school. Maria changed her shoes and tidied her hair, and then she set out for the dog pound in the town.

Paco had not relished the task of executing the culprits in the cave, the less so because it was followed the next day by a reprimand from the Mayor. The whole bad business, it seemed, was being blamed on him. The boys who had let the dogs out of the pound had confessed to the deed, but both of them – questioned separately – were denying that they had got in by forcing the lock as alleged. They declared, and their story could not be shaken, that they had found the barn door unlocked.

'If you are capable of such carelessness you are not fit to hold the important post of dog-catcher in this town,' said Don Anselmo severely. 'The consequences might have been a good deal worse. Imagine what would have happened if a tourist, for instance, had been attacked by those savage brutes! I'll say no more now, but I trust this won't occur again.'

'You may rest assured it won't, your honour.'

Paco looked suitably repentant when he left the town hall, but inwardly he was fuming. The only reason he had left the accursed door unlocked was because he had been worn out after that long walk out to the cottage and back – and he with his bad leg. Oh, it was unfair, unfair.

He was still in a very bad temper when Maria arrived with Pepito, the indirect cause of Paco's tribulations. After listening to her account of the rescue, he said sulkily, 'All right, you can leave him here. I've got enough to do, heaven knows, but one more won't make any difference.' And he dragged Pepito roughly inside, tied him to a ring bolt between two other dogs and left him there on a heap of musty straw.

9

Paco's ill temper had gone the next morning, giving place to a mood of depression. He went to work reluctantly. This would be another bad day so far as he was concerned. Yesterday there was the shooting, today the vet's visit. He would have to give the pound a thorough turn out because Carlos was a fussy man and might report him if he did not find the place as clean as he considered it should be.

Furiously raking up the soiled straw Paco paused at the spot where Pepito lay with his eyes fixed on the doorway, waiting for someone to come and fetch him out of this strange dark place, someone whose voice still rang in his ears, at whose heels he had trotted till his pads were sore, in whose bed-roll he had slept on many a night under the pines. His appearance now belied him. He was no longer the comical little fellow he had been then, full of bounce and fun. The fun had been crushed out of him together with the vitality and confidence – but not the hope. Through that door might come – *must come* – sooner or later the figure of his god and master.

Paco stared down at him, 'Poor little beggar,' he thought. 'Looks as if he's been through a rough time lately. Wonder who he belonged to?' Whoever it was didn't deserve such devotion. That steadfast look spoke volumes. 'He's waiting for someone who'll never come.' But there was no time to get sentimental. He wasn't nearly ready yet for Carlos, who might arrive at any hour between now and lunchtime, having to fit this job in among his other calls. He was the only vet in the district and constantly in demand.

Paco was not squeamish. He would not have taken his present job if he had been. But the part of it that he hated was separating the dogs who were to be put down from those who would be kept a little longer. The choice was his and it put him in the position of judge and executioner. It was not difficult to make. The animals who had a chance of adoption were the best-looking ones with some pretensions to breeding. The old, the sick and ugly, did not warrant the cost of their keep.

He walked round with a frowning face making his selection. A very old spaniel, nearly blind, was the first to be tethered at the far end of the barn where Carlos worked, and then, a couple of mongrels with colitis. It was hard to cure disease when there was no allowance for medicines on a dog-catcher's pay and Carlos could not spare time to attend to them. After these he picked a grey poodle, pretty enough to look at, but vicious. She had been adopted once and brought back again when her vicious tendencies were discovered. A child had been bitten through the thumb.

Now he was back again, staring at Pepito. What chance had this bedraggled little animal – with the bare patch on his side where the fur had been torn out – and it would take a long time to grow back – of finding a home when there were attractive dogs for the taking? None, he decided. None whatever. He led Pepito down to the end of the barn and tied him between the old spaniel and a basketful of unwanted puppies.

99

It was his practice to bring a bag of sweet biscuits on these days for distribution among the condemned. They were all very quiet, as was invariably the case. Did they know? He was more than half convinced that they did, despite what was said to the contrary. He handed round the biscuits, which were eaten with enjoyment by all except Pepito, who refused the offering. Paco stooped to fondle him. He might as well have fondled a block of wood for all the response he evoked. 'It's no use, chiquito, can't you understand? He's not coming. No one has been here to look for you. No one wants you. No one is coming.'

But Paco was wrong. At the very time when he was talking to Pepito, the young Frenchman had already been released with apologies from the city police for the unfortunate mistake which had been made and the inconvenience he had been caused, and was on his way back to San Agustin.

Jean-Louis's first thought when he left the gaol was for Pepito. He knew that he ought to wait till his money came through. After buying cigarettes, a new pair of sandals and a good breakfast he had very little left. But he felt within him a pressing urgency – something telling him to hurry back to San Agustin as quickly as he could. Pepito was there, somewhere in this neighbourhood still; of that he felt certain. But he had been told that Pepito was not in the dog pound. So – where was he? Had someone taken him in? The town was a small place where news would spread rapidly. Somebody might know. He hadn't enough money for the train fare so he had to get there as best he could, by bus and by hitch-hiking. Before leaving the city he went to the bank recommended to him by the Honorary Consul and asked that when his money came it should be forwarded to the branch in San Agustin.

There are times in life when everything works out well, and other times when it seems as if the whole world is against you and nothing goes right. Jean-Louis's journey that day was a good example of the second kind of occasion. It did not seem to present much difficulty at the outset, but it proved to be both complicated and vexatious. To start with, he did not find it easy to get a lift down the motorway to the point at which he would pick up the bus. This obstacle had not occurred to him. On previous holidays in Spain he had crossed whole provinces by hitching rides on long distance lorries. At that time drivers would willingly stop to pick up a friendly-looking traveller. Theirs is a lonely life and they were glad of company. Now things were different. By new regulations they were forbidden to give lifts. Only a few were willing to take the risk of a fine or prosecution. Consequently Jean-Louis had to wait a long time at the entry to the motorway before a delivery truck loaded with sacks of flour pulled up beside him. The driver was a young man of about his own age. After carefully scanning the road both ways for a police patrol he said, 'Hop in!' and Jean-Louis quickly climbed up into the cab.

They had not gone many miles before the engine started to misbehave. There was a knocking noise and steam gushed from the radiator. They pulled up in a lay-by while the driver got out to investigate, and Jean-Louis fumed with impatience, wondering if he ought to leave the truck and try for a lift in a more reliable vehicle. But he knew that nothing is allowed to stop on a motorway except in the case of a break-down. To walk back to the point at which he joined the truck would take him an hour or more, and he would then have to wait all over again for the advent of another willing driver. It would be better to stay with the present one and try to control his impatience. 'What's wrong?' he asked.

'Nothing much. A loose fan belt, that's all. Have to change it – but I carry a spare. See if you can find it, will you? Look in that box at the back of the cab.'

Fitting the new fan belt did not take long. But it was then necessary to wait until the overheated engine cooled down before they could go on. Then there was a puncture in one of the rear tyres. 'You're bad luck, you are, mate,' said the driver. 'I never had no trouble with this old girl before. Now she's let me down twice. I don't know as I dare take you any further in case she falls to bits!'

Jean-Louis would have liked nothing better than to leave at this point; but had he done so his position would have been hopeless, for they were now in the middle of a long section of motorway. At least he could do something to help this time, instead of sitting fuming in the cab. Two can change a tyre more quickly than one. The driver by this time was aware of his impatience. 'In a hurry, are you?'

'Yes.'

'What's the trouble?'

'I would like to tell you – but I speak Spanish so badly. I am French, you see.'

'Tell me in French then.'

'You speak it?'

'No, but I understand it pretty well. I have a French girl friend. She works in a hostel.'

'That's marvellous.' So Jean-Louis told his story. At the end he said, 'I have this feeling, you see, that unless I get back quickly I might as well not go at all. Something tells me that Pepito is alive but in danger.'

'What kind of a dog is he?'

'Oh, nothing to look at. A mixture of half a dozen different breeds. But he deserves to have a home and I want to give him one. Can we go a bit faster?'

'We'll try. I'm fond of dogs myself. But I can't take you all the way, you know that. I'll drop you on the bus route to Lodosa –'

'To Lodosa? But I want to go to San Agustin!'

'You can't, not by bus, so far as I know.'

'But they told me –'

'I can't help what they told you. You should have taken the train in the first place.'

'This is awful. What can I do?'

'It's not so bad. Listen. You take the Lodosa bus to where the road forks to San Agustin, and you hitch another ride from there. OK?'

'OK,' said Jean-Louis, 'and thanks.'

He caught the bus at the end of the motorway and left it at the branch road to San Agustin. He sat on a wall and waited for a goods van or a car with an empty seat. Nothing came by. Nothing at all. He couldn't understand it – until he walked back a little way and saw what he hadn't noticed when leaving the bus. There was a 'Road up' sign, and below it another sign saying 'Diversion' with an arrow pointing down the motorway. It was no use working himself into a state again. 'Calm down,' he said to himself, 'and do the only thing you can do. *Walk*.' 'Oh well,' he thought, 'it won't do me any harm after being cooped up in that cell.'

With his pack on his back and both arms free he swung along at a brisk pace and soon came to the section where the road work was going on. A long stretch of the surface had been newly laid and the heavy roller was grinding to and fro. The men called out a greeting as Jean-Louis strode by.

It was a grand day for walking, with a strong breeze that tempered the heat. Maize was being harvested in the fields bordering the road. The sight of some dogs romping among the harvesters set Jean-Louis to thinking about Pepito. He had no clear plan to put into operation when he reached San Agustin. The town was strange to him. He had merely been passing through it when he was arrested. Perhaps the first thing he ought to do was to go to the police station. But by now they would have informed him if they had any news of his dog. They would be only too anxious to make some amends for the ordeal he had been through. He did not want to waste time, and anyway he had had enough of policemen for the time being. It was not that they had treated him badly. But being arrested on a wrongful charge is a nasty thing to happen to a holiday-maker in a foreign country. No, he would do better to go to the restaurant where the trouble started and make inquiries there, and in neighbouring bars and cafés.

After an hour's steady walking he had to stop. The new sandals were chafing his feet and he wished he had kept the old ones. There were blisters on several of his toes and they needed attention. He had to take off his pack and empty it to find the small first aid kit, and having found it discovered that it was short of adhesive plaster. He had to do something or his feet would be raw and it would be too painful to walk at all. He took out his clean shirt and tore the tail of it into strips with which he bound his toes. Then, of course, the sandals were too tight and the pressure alone was painful, but he hobbled on as fast as he could.

He came to a cross-road and a signpost. There was still a long way to go and his pace had slowed considerably. He began to wonder if he would ever reach San Agustin.

Carlos had only one call to make that morning and, had things gone as planned, he would have got to the pound a good deal earlier than he actually did. The visit was to a farm where a valuable cow was due to calve. She had had many calves before without trouble but now she was getting old and this time the birth was difficult. The farmer was not rich and he had hesitated to call on the services of a vet until it was clear that he had no choice. The two men did what they could to help the cow, but it seemed as if the calf didn't want to be born. Hours went by until at last, to their huge relief, the little creature was there safe and sound, trying to stand on its feeble legs while its mother licked it clean.

After all this it was unthinkable that Carlos should not be invited into the house and offered a drink to celebrate the event. It was, therefore, very near midday when he left the farm and he had seven kilometres to cover in his old yellow Citroën to reach the dog pound at San Agustin. He wanted to get the job done and be home punctually for lunch because his brother-in-law was coming and they had some business to discuss. He had to hurry. When he saw a young man standing by the roadside signalling that he wanted a lift, Carlos did not stop.

The young man was Jean-Louis. He had stopped again to rest and was looking up and down the empty road, longing for the sight of a vehicle of any sort, when he suddenly saw a car turn out of a farm entrance a short way back. He stood up and waved. The driver shook his head and drove right past him, going so fast that his shabby old car rattled and thumped. Jean-Louis sat down again and adjusted the bandages on his sore toes. No other car came by. There was nothing for it but to press on.

The sun was high overhead and the big clock in the square was striking one when he limped into town. He was very thirsty and took a long drink from the fountain under the plane trees. Then he made for the nearest chemist's shop where the pharmacist put antiseptic dressings on his blisters. After this he went to the Restaurant Marisol.

He asked for the proprietor and explained who he was and why he had come. Señor Cardona, who spoke a little French, was both apologetic and helpful. 'It was most unfortunate, what happened here. I hope you will find it possible to forgive and forget. Let me tell you at once that the waiter who denounced you has left my service, so you will not suffer the unpleasantness of meeting him. And now may I offer you some lunch?'

'No, thank you, I –'

'Please, as my guest.'

'It's kind of you but I can't spare the time now. Some other day perhaps. I'm looking for my dog. He was with me that day and got left behind when I was taken away.'

'I don't remember a dog –'

'He's very small. A sort of terrier. Black and white.'

Señor Cardona had a practical turn of mind. He seated Jean-Louis at a table with an aperitif and a pen and paper and asked him to make a sketch. Jean-Louis was not very good at drawing but he managed to produce a rough like-ness of Pepito which the proprietor took to each table in turn, asking, 'Have you seen a dog like this?'

One by one the customers shook their heads and finally Señor Cardona returned the drawing to Jean-Louis. He said, 'I think you should try the dog pound.'

'The police have made inquiries there.'

'When did they do so?'

'A day or two ago. I was informed of this shortly before the order came for my release.'

'But I don't think you quite understand. Dogs are being impounded all the time, wherever they are found on the streets. Just because yours was not there at the time of the inquiry, it does not follow that he is not there today. He could have been picked up last night. I think you should go to the pound, and –' Señor Cardona looked at his watch – 'you had better go quickly.' He did not explain why, and Jean-Louis wasted no more time but took his advice and went out to find the pound.

It was half past one when he finally found it and then he was not sure if he had come to the right place. From a distance it looked like a large barn. But as he drew near it he could hear the howling and yelping of dogs. Outside the building stood the yellow Citroën that had passed him on the road.

He ran to the barn door and tried the handle. The door seemed to be bolted on the inside. He peered through the window. In the dust and gloom of the interior he saw two men at work, one with grey hair and an eye patch, the other younger, among the dogs that strained and tugged at their ropes trying to get away from them. In a corner, half covered with straw, were some that did not move at all. Jean-Louis understood then why he had been advised to hurry. He thumped on the window to attract the men's attention, but they could not hear him. He saw the younger man, who had some sort of instrument in his hand, seize one of the cowering dogs, a very small one, by the loose skin at the back of its neck. He saw its black-and-white face, its frightened eyes – and his efforts to draw attention to himself became frantic. He rattled the bars over the window, then picked up a stone and hit the window between the bars so hard that he shattered the glass. Both men turned and stared as Jean-Louis yelled at the top of his voice in French, '*C'est mon chien! Ne le touchez pas!*'

The older man smiled and said something to the other. A minute later Pepito was in his master's arms.

Not long afterwards Jean-Louis was once again waiting at the roadside for a lift. His feet were still too sore for much walking. His money had come and he had booked a flight to Paris on a Spanish airline. Pepito sat on the pavement beside him, wearing a red leather collar with brass studs. His coat was sleek again and his eyes were bright and happy. A car pulled up, and the driver waved a cheerful greeting. It was Señor Cardona of the restaurant.

'You found him, then?'

'Yes, just in time. I'm grateful that you warned me to hurry. A few more minutes and I would have been too late.'

'Can I give you a lift anywhere?'

'To the station, please, if it's not too much trouble. I have to get to the airport.' Jean-Louis climbed in and sat on the front seat with Pepito on his knees.

'I didn't like to tell you this,' said Señor Cardona as

they drove along, 'but Don Carlos, the vet, is a friend of mine. We belong to the same club. I'm familiar with his movements and I knew that he was due for a visit that morning. Well, I'm glad you are reunited with your dog. That's a smart collar he's wearing.'

'Yes, but he objected at first. It may be the first time in his life that he has worn one, and he regarded it as an indignity. Now I think he rather likes it.'

'No doubt he does. He realizes it is a badge of rank, to be envied by less fortunate animals.'

Pepito wriggled round so that he could watch the passing traffic, revealing the scar on his side.

'How did he come by that, do you know?' asked Señor Cardona.

'No, I don't,' said Jean-Louis. 'He must have had many adventures during the time we were separated. I know that he was very nearly shot and that he fell down a well and was rescued by the dog-catcher's cousin. When I get home I shall send her a present.'

'That's a kind thought. Well, here we are at the station. This is the end of a chapter for you, and the start of a new life for one little dog. Goodbye, young man. I hope you are both going to be very happy.'

Pepito had no more adventures. The rest of his life, which was a long one, passed in tranquil contentment.

After they were married Jean-Louis and Chantal moved from Paris to a house in a small town in Provence where the young man had been offered a legal post.

The house was on the edge of the town and beyond it lay a stretch of wild country where Jean-Louis and Pepito took their evening walks. It reminded them both of Spain. There were the same scented herbs and basking lizards. There were rabbits to chase. And sometimes Pepito would try to catch a rook or a pigeon as he used to do when he hunted with Tigre. But he had grown plumper with good living and could no longer leap so high. Nor was he quite so energetic. He was eight years old now.

After Chantal had her baby he was content to walk sedately beside the pram, guarding it from anyone who came too close.

The couple were still living in the same house many years later, after other babies had come. But now the pram had a new guardian. In the garden was a flat grey stone engraved with the words:

HIS NAME WAS PEPITO.
HE WAS THE FRIEND OF
JEAN-LOUIS AND CHANTAL
LEBLANC.